Psycho Husband

Kenneth Bilbao

Copyright © 2024 by Kenneth Bilbao

All rights reserved.

No portion of this book may be reproduced in any form without written permission from the publisher or author, except as permitted by U.S. copyright law.

Contents

1. prologue — 1
2. Meet Mr. Wilson Mike. — 3
3. His reality — 12
4. Medicines — 24
5. PYSCO — 38
6. I am scared — 49
7. His truth — 62
8. Let's go out. — 73
9. A beautiful night — 84
10. Party — 95
11. She is drunk — 109
12. confess. — 121
13. love — 132
14. kidnap — 143
15. plan — 156

16. Damon	168
17. I will kill him	181
18. A new member	196
19. Hate me	208
20. Letter	223
21. Avery	231
22. Lisa	242
23. Hide	253
24. Back to home	266
25. Reunion	279
26. Trip	296

prologue

" I love you " He said while smiling and coming towards me. I started to take back steps. My eyes is full of tears. I am shivering and scared to see him. Suddenly I got hit by wall. I am about to escape. He pulled me and pinned to wall.

" AH.... " I yelled loudly. His danger eyes, His Smile, His voice making me scare more. His touch. I am literally shivering more and more. He slowly placed his hand on my face. My eyes rolled towards his hand.

No.... No... No... please.... leave me.

" Are you okay ? Why are you crying ? " He said in sad tone. I started to cry badly.

" Don't cry " He said calmly wiping my tears. He started to stare at me. He is so close to me. I ignored him and just crying with all my heart.

" I said don't cry " He said a little anger in his voice. He removed his hands from me and placed his both hands on his head.

He is about to get angry.

" DON'T CRY !!!! " This time he shouted so loudly. My heart stopped a second. He hit the wall with his hand angrily. His hand is bleeding.

" I... I... can't see you cry. I won't let you cry. No...No.... I... love you.. I love you " I seen a vibration in his voice. small tears are in his eyes.

This is not a love. It is mad.

" You are mine " He said and smiled at me. He took my hand. I am so scared of him. I am about to take back my hand. He looked at me angrily. He pulled my hand to him. He started to stare at wedding ring. He slowly kissed my ring. A shiver hit in my heart.

" My wife " He said smiling at me and pulled me into a tight hug. I closed my eyes tightly and started to cry.

This is not love. It's physco.

YOU ARE A PHYSCO !!!!!

MR. WILSON MIKE !!!!!

Meet Mr. Wilson Mike.

A very point of view

As I opened my eyes. I seen myself on bed naked. And a pair of arms wrapped around me.

A tear rolled in my eyes.

Why ? Why ? Why it's happening to me ?

I started to stare my husband.

He is handsome. He looks just awesome. But.... But.... He scares me. I don't like him.

If it not because of my little brother I wouldn't have married him.

Suddenly he opened his eyes.

The minute he opened his bright eyes. My heart started to beat. I am almost started to sweat. My lips left dry. I lowered my eyes.

He slowly placed his hand on my face. I shivered quickly.

" Why are you shivering ? " He asked. I literally sensed his anger voice. I hold my fist tightly.

No.... No.... Why did you shivered Avery ? Now face the consequences.

" Are you scared of me ? " He asked angrily and pulled my wrist tightly.

That's it tears appeared in my eyes.

" AH.... " I whispered in pain. He started to press tightly. Tear rolled down my cheek.

" N_o " I said in tears. In a second he released his hand. I seen my wrist has his finger marks it's turned into red.

" Don't cry " He said in sad tone and wiped my tears with his rough thumb. I stopped in a second.

If I don't stop I know what will happen.

He not only harms me but also harms himself. It's scares me.

" Get dressed " He said while smiling and got up. He gave me my clothes which where all over the floor. He got up and started to wear his underwear and his short pants. I sat on bed covering myself with blanket.

" Do you need my help ? " He asked while staring at me. He is shirtless.

He has a great 6 pack muscles. But.... He looks good from appearance but from inside he is just a devil.

Just a PYSCO

" I.... " Before I speak. He came to me and pulled the blanket away from me. My eyes widen in shock. I quickly wrapped my arms to cover myself. He took my underwear and started to put on me.

Why ? It's like a hell. It's feels like I sat on thrones.

It's embrassing. I never showed my body to anybody. It's so bold. Even he is my husband. I don't like him.

He took my bra and started to put on me. I just lowered my eyes. I even can't able to cry wholeheartedly.

He started to put my night pants and shirt on me. He done dressing me and looked at me.

" My wife " He smiled. I hardly looked at him. He placed a kiss on my forehead.

" Go and take bath " He said placing his hand on my head. And got off the bed.

Ron.... I have to ask him where did he hide Ron ?

Ron is my younger brother. He is 5 years old. He is my life and everything. After our parents died he is the only one I have in my life.

" Mike " I called his name for the first time.

" Yes " He said and turned to me while smiling.

" I... Want to see Ron " I asked hesitatly. Suddenly his face turned into anger.

" I said you to take bath " He said angrily and opened his eyes widely. I hold the blanket tightly in fear.

No... I can't take this. I am serious about Ron. If anything happens to him I can't able to live.

I took a deep breath.

" He... Will be scared without seeing me " I said in sad tone.

That's all. Now see his anger.

You are really a idiot Avery.

He came to me and in a second he hopped on the bed and pulled my hair hardly.

" AH.... " I yelled in pain.

" TAKE BATH !!! " He shouted loudly. His eyes are red in anger.

" It's.... Paining " I said in tears. Suddenly he changed in a second.

" Why you make me angry ? You know right I can't see you cry " He said in sad tone.

In a second he hugged me tightly. I started to breath hardly. I am shivering in his arms. He broke the hug and quickly wiped my tears.

" Go. Take bath " He said while smiling while placing his hands on my face. I gave a quick nod while shivering and ran into the washroom. I quickly locked the door. I started to on all the taps. I on the shower and collapsed on ground. I placed my both hands on my mouth and started to cry. The warm water hitting my cold body.

Did he do something to Ron ?

I cried and cried for 10 minutes. I just sat there without a life in my body. My head started to pain. I am about to place my hand on my head. I noticed my wedding ring on my finger. I closed my eyes tears dropped down my cheek.

2 days back.

" Sis, I am hungry " Ron said in sad tone placing his hand on stomach.

I earn a little money and we don't even have a food to eat daily.

I want to place Ron in a reputed school.

We live in a every small room. My earned money goes on rent and bills.

I even can't able to make Ron Happy. I can't give him toys, clothes. Even.... A delicious food.

I placed two bread slices and stuffed a jam between. And ran to Ron and started to feed him. He quickly started to eat it.

It's been 10 hours. I worked in a store and brought this bread to feed him. A tear rolled in my eyes.

" Sis, Eat " He said while giving his bright smile and placed the bread to my mouth. I took a bite.

" Yehhh....... I have food today " Ron said excitingly and clapped his both hands. I smiled.

" Sis, Look I draw the picture of our family " Ron said showing me his drawing.

I seen he draw out mother, father me and him in it.

" Wow !!! Our Ron has grown up. I will buy you a chocolate today " I said.

" Really ? " Ron said and started to jump. I nodded.

" Sis, When I will go to school ? " He asked in sad tone. A pain hit in my heart.

I controlled my tears.

" Soon. You will be going to a big school. Where you can play, learn and have a lots of fun and wear nice clothes " I said while placing a smile.

I hope this will be true.

" Yehh... I will learn and earn lots of money and will be living in a big house " He said. I quickly pulled into a tight hug. Tears rolled down my cheek.

" Of course My Ron can do anything " I said and wiped my tears. I broke the hug and placed a kiss on his little cheek.

" Now be a good boy and stay at home. Sis has to go for work. " I said tapping his head. He nodded and smiled. I got up and about to turn. I looked at Ron.

" So, What are the rules when I leave home to work ? " I asked him. He raised his hand and started to count and say.

" 1. Don't open the door and go out..

2. If anybody knocks don't open the door.

3. If I am feeling ill I should call you. " He said. I smiled.

" And... The last one " I asked. He started to think.

" Don't make room messy " I said and gave a small hit on his forehead.

" Ouch !!! I know sis " He said rubbing his head. I laughed and I walked towards the door and made sure the door is locked correctly and came out of the building.

Suddenly I seen some people are disturbing pamphlets. One man ran to me and gave me the pamphlet.

I looked into it.

" We need workers

Salary : 139$ "

Place : Montcalm luxury 5 star hotel

Timings : 9:00pm - 12:00am "

Wow !!! Looks like a rich job. I had to attend the interview.

But... Looks like night shifts.

Then.... Ron.

I will put him in kinder garden for a mean while. After earning for sometime I can take him to work.

....

It's 9:00pm. I hardly put Ron in kinder garden. He kept on crying. But some how I managed.

I stood in front of the luxury hotel. My eyes widen seeing the beauty of the hotel.

Looks like rich people's place.

I looked at my dress which is just normal. It doesn't suit this place.

I slowly walked towards the door. I seen security saluted me. I gave a nod and walked inside. My mouth widen seeing the interior.

It's just like a heaven.

I seen the reception. I walked to it and I seen a women in her uniform. She is just so beautiful and see looks like a angel.

" What can I do for you Mam ? " She asked smiling at me. I gave her the pamphlet. Suddenly I seen her face turned into a disgust. She looked at me from top to bottom.

Looks like I don't suit this place.

" This way " She said showing me the direction. I started to walk towards that direction.

" Are you looking for job ? " I heard a man spoke. He wore a black suit. He is 6 feet.

Looks like a bodyguard.

I gave a nod. He guided me into the lift. I walked into the lift. He pressed the top floor.

As we reached the top floor. I seen a receptionist there.

" She is the new worker here " The Man said who came with me in lift. The receptionist nodded.

" This way " she said taking me. I seen there are lots of rooms. She swiped a card to one of the room.

" Get inside " She said. I nodded and got inside.

" Please wait here I will inform you " She said and walked out. I started to explore the room. Suddenly I found a bunch of condoms in a small basket on table.

Condoms ?

I also seen a medicines. And a disgusting reveling clothes on bed.

I think I came into a wrong place.

My eyes widen in shock. I am about to go out. Suddenly I heard a door sound. I seen a mam coming into the room.

He is 6 feet and looking at him he as 6 pack and his hair is back. His eyes are back.

He looked at me.

Flash back ends.

" Do you want me to join ? " Suddenly I heard his voice. I opened my eyes quickly.

Hey guys here the first episode. Hope you guys like it.

Please do like share and comment.

Thank you.

His reality

Mike point of view

Come on !!!

Kill him !!!

Kill him !!!

Kill him !!!

" NO !!!! " I yelled loudly and got up. I am sweating and breathing hardly.

Same dream again.

Why this dream is killing me from inside ?

I got out of the bed and went into the washroom and started to shower. Tears rolled in my eyes.

The pain which I am hiding myself from all this year's.

Why this second person in me making me evil ?

As I took warm shower. I came out of the bathroom. I pulled a my phone.

" I want women Tonight " I said on phone. The minute I hung up the call. I seen my phone started ringing.

Doctor ?

I quickly picked up the call.

" Hello Mr Wilson Mike. How are you feeling right now ? " He asked.

I have been going through treatment for past 20 years.

" Just as it is " I said in frustration.

" Are you taking the medicines ? " He asked. I walked towards my draw. I seen bunch of tablets bottles are still there.

" Sir, It's your medicines time " My servant said giving me my medicine. The minute I looked into it. My eyes turned into red. I throwed the tablets of ground angrily.

" KEEP THEM AWAY FROM ME " I shouted loudly in anger. I landed on floor and started to yell loudly.

" AH.... AH.... AH.... " Seeing me yelling my servant got scared and ran from there.

I started to beat my head hardly with my hands. Tears rolling in my eyes.

" GET OUT OF THE HEAD.... please " I yelled in pain and started to cry loudly.

I don't have friends, family. I don't have anyone who belongs to me. And this disease is killing me from inside.

" Mike , are you there ? " I came out of my thoughts.

" Yes " I said blinking my eyes.

" How about you come to hospital ? I am going to take some tests for you " He said.

" I will " I said and nodded and hung up the call. I heard a door knock.

" Come in " I said. My servant came into the room.

His name is Jack. He always been there with me from past 9 years. Seeing my disease he is so scared of me that he will never get close to me.

" Sir... This are the profiles of women's for you today " He said giving me a file. I took the files and started to look at each women.

Same again.

I throwed the files of ground angrily.

" Same again. Not even a single women as the boldness I am looking for. I want a women to sleep with me for a night. Did you get that ? " He said angrily. He placed his head down.

" But.... Sir this are the top prostitutes " He said in scared. He is almost shivering.

" I said bold " I repeated.

" Can... You describe bold sir ? So, that I can bring you more women's " He said hesitatly.

I want a woman who I can rest my head on her shoulder.

" Tell the company that I personally get there to pick a women " I said. He quickly nodded and walked out of the room.

....

" Sir, Pl_ease... Listen to us " The worker said in fear.

" I TOLD YOU TO SHOW BOLD GIRLS " I yelled loudly in anger.

" Si_r.... This are top girls in our company " He said showing me the bunch of girls stood in front of me almost naked. I quickly pulled his collar angrily.

" Sir, A new girl as just came " Some guy came running to us. I loosen his shirt. He started to cough.

" This way sir " He said showing me the way.

" If I don't accept this girl. I am going to close your company " I said angrily and walked to that direction.

The minute I opened the door. My eyes met with a beautiful girl in front of me.

She is just so beautiful. Her skin is just like a pure milk. Her eyes. Her lips. She is so short.

The minute she looked at me. She got scared and moved back.

" I.... Came into the wrong place " She said and about to go. In a second I pulled her wrist. And pinned her to the nearest wall. I started to stare at her face closely. A smile appeared on my face. I am about to touch her face. Suddenly she slapped on my cheek.

The inner devil in me woke up.

I looked at her angrily. And pulled her jaw tightly.

" YOU ARE MINE " I yelled loudly pressing her jaw. Tears rolled in her eyes.

....

Avery point of view

Where is Ron ? I want to see him. I can't able to live without him.

Why this PYSCO blackmailed me and married me ?

" Sis " suddenly I heard Ron voice. As I turned around I seen Ron came running to me.

Ron ? When did he got here ?

" Ron " I said and kneeled down and hugged him tightly.

It's just 1 day still I can't be without him even a second.

I started to look at him. Did that PYSCO do something to him or not ?

" Are you hurt anywhere ? Did they scared you ? Are you hungry ? They did'nt gave you food right ? " I started to ask all the question at a time.

" Sis , I had a lot of fun " He said waving his hands on air.

" Huh ? " I am just so confused.

Mike didn't do anything to him ?

Suddenly he took his little back pack from his shoulder. And started to show something to me.

" Sis, Look. They gave a chocolates, Toys, Books and... " Ron keeping on saying while taking all the stuff from the bag.

" Who gave you all this ? " I asked in shock.

" Me " Suddenly I heard a voice. As I turned around I seen Mike stood there. He wore his causal wear. The voice which scared me last night.

His voice, His anger, His presence, His eyes.... Everything Made me scared last night.

It's a bad nightmare to me.

I never call it as a first night of ours.

I quickly pulled Ron and hide him behind me. He started to look at Ron.

No, Don't hurt him. I can take this anger but he is kid he can't handle this PYSCO.

" Ron, Come here " Mike said while smiling. I hold his hand tightly. I started to sweat and shiver. He seen that I am holding Ron's hand tightly. His grace on me making me scare.

" Ron, Come here " He said and opened his arms while smiling.

" Sis, Who is he ? " Ron asked softly and a little scared. I am about to answer him.

" When you come here I am going to tell you " Mike said and pulled a chocolate from his blazer. In a second Ron ran to him.

" RON !!! " I called his name loudly. I went behind him. Mike quickly lifted him in his arms. Ron pulled the chocolate from his hand.

" Thank you " Ron said and he is about to eat.

No... He might poisoned the chocolate.

" DON'T EAT " I shouted loudly and quickly throwed the chocolate on the ground. Suddenly Ron started to cry.

He will kill us Ron. He is PYSCO. After last night I came to know his real face. He is not a person as he looks.

Mike looked at me angrily.

You can harm me but not Ron please.

I pulled Ron from his arms. He is crying so badly.

I never seen him crying. Tears rolled in my eyes.

" I... Am sorry. " I said tapping his back slowly. Tears rolled down my cheek. I looked at Mike he as a different expression in his face.

" Why are you crying ? " He asked wiping my tears. I moved back in a second. Ron keeps on crying.

" He made you cry right ? " He looked at Ron angrily.

No !!!

No !!!

If he sees me crying because of him. He will kill Ron.

" NO !!! I.... I.... Got something in my eyes " I said and quickly wiped my tears.

" Let me blow it " He said coming closer to my face.

" I hate you " suddenly Ron said in tears. Mike moved back.

He never said I hate you to me.

Why are you making complex Ron ?

Why did you said I hate you to me ?

Mike Hates when somebody says I hate you to me.

" Please..... Don't do anything to him. He is my brother. He is still kid " I started to beg him. And hugged him tightly.

" I will buy you another big chocolate " He said patting the Ron's head.

" Uncle " Ron said in sad tone and opened his arms to go to Mike. He took Ron quickly in his arms. And wiped his tears.

" If your sister loves you this much then I love you more than her. I love everything what your sister loves " He said to Ron looking at me. I let out the breath.

" Are we going to stay here from now on ? " Ron asked.

" Of course. This entire house belongs to us. You can do anything nobody will say anything to you " Mike said smiling at Ron. I just stood listening to their conversation.

" Really ? Sis, Then I can go to school right ? " Ron asked in excitement.

Before I reply.

" Yes, From now on I am your uncle. I married your sister. So, Be as you like in this house " He said. Ron clapped in excitement.

" I want to see the house " Ron said.

" Go " Mike said and placed Ron on ground. He started to run.

" Ron, Don't go far " I said in concerned.

" Don't worry there is cameras everywhere so, no one can escape from this house " He said in his voice again.

He is not the person I seen last night. Last night is just so horrible to me.

" Do you know how to make breakfast ? " Mike asked smiling at me. I gave a quick nod.

" How about you make me breakfast ? I want to taste your food. " He said in soft voice.

Am I seeing the same person ? He looks just opposite to the person which I seen last night.

" What ? " He asked waving his hand in front of me. I came out of my thoughts and gave a nod.

....

I am in kitchen trying to see what to cook.

What food he likes ? If I make something and he don't like I don't want to see his anger again.

There is no single servant in this house. After I got married he dragged me into this house from then I didn't see a person in this house.

How Ron came here ? Where did he hide him on last night ? Ron not even crying and looks happy ?

" Do you want me to help ? " Suddenly I heard his voice. I came out of thoughts. I didn't replied to him and quickly started to search the pan.

" It's in second cupboard " He said pointing me the cupboard. I took the pan and placed it stove.

I opened the fridge and picked up eggs, Milk, Bread.

I looked at Mike he keep on staring at me.

I ignored him and started to beat the eggs.

Suddenly I don't know what happened to me. Mike pulled my head and started to kiss me.

His lips crashed my lips and he started to kiss so passionately.

I can't even cry in front of him.

The kiss sounds making the room more hot.

After a few minutes he stopped kissing and looked at my face.

" Why are you so beautiful ? " He asked on my lips. He gave a kiss again on my lips.

His stare is just so different.

He is not mike. The Mike I seen last night is cruel, Evil, Danger.

He took my ear in his mouth. His wet touched my ear. which made me shiver.

" Why are you shivering ? " He asked and Frowned his eyebrows.

I am scared of you. I don't know when your evil will be back.

" It's.... It's.... Tickles " I said. He laughed.

He is laughing ? I didn't see him laugh.

This guy is just so question mark.

" Sis " Suddenly I heard Ron voice. Mike got separated from me.

" Sis, This house is so beautiful " Ron said while smiling. I smiled at him.

" Then hurry and pack your bag. I am going to drop you in school " Mike said.

School ? He already joined Ron in school ? He didn't informed me.

" Yehhh..... I can go to school now " Ron said and ran out of kitchen.

" Come on !!! Ron will be hungry " He said. My eyes widen in shock.

He is talking casually.

He walked out of the room. I started to prepare the breakfast.

After half an hour. I placed all the dishes on dinning table. Suddenly I seen Ron and Mike playing.

They became friends. I smiled looking at them.

Suddenly my eyes caught his tattoos. I am so scared last night that I didn't seen anything.

He as tattoos. I am scared last night and early tomorrow. That I didn't concentrated on his body.

" Breakfast is ready " I said. Mike and Ron both looked at me and came and sat on chairs. I eyes are just seeing his tattoos.

Every tattoos on his body looks so different and strange.

While he is eating I started to read them slowly while eating.

" Don't kill "

" Don't harm anybody "

" Happiness is having family "

" Kill the PYSCO..... " Before I read further.

" Aren't you eating ? " Suddenly I heard his voice. I came out of thoughts. He looked that I am seeing his tattoos.

Suddenly he got up from chair.

" I will be back " He said. And walked inside.

He is gone do something to me that I read his tattoos ?

I started to shiver and scared. I seen Ron who is busy in eating. My eyes are on upstairs.

After a few minutes I seen him coming down.

He changed his clothes. He wore full sleeves to cover the tattoos.

My eyes widen in shock. What's secrets are hiding on his body ?

Medicines

A very point of view

" Delicious " Suddenly Mike said eating the food.

" Huh ? " I asked in confused.

I thought he is going to kill me for seeing his tattoos.

" Sis Makes delicious pancake. It's my favorite " Ron said eating them.

"Everything she makes or do just perfect " He said looking into my eyes.

What's got into him ? I mean he is different.

" I am done. Let me drop you in school " Mike said smiling at Ron. Ron pulled his bag and stood up.

No, I can't let him be alone with Ron. He is dangerous.

" I will come too " I said. Ron looked at me and nodded.

....

Again in the same room. Ron went to school. I am so happy that he is going to school.

I am scared here. I am really scared.

Seeing him scared me.

" Good morning Mam " suddenly I heard a voice. As I turned my head I seen a mam stood there.

He is around 40's. He has white hair. Looks like servant.

" Yes, Please come in " I said and stood from bed.

I never seen a single servant then who is he ? Nobody can enter here without Mike's permission.

" I am jack Mike's personal assistant. I have been working here for past 11 years. " He introduced himself.

11 years ? My God !!! How can he tolerate Mike for 11 years ?

" Mam, Here are the important medicines. You should give this to sir " He said handing me a packet of medicines.

Medicines ? He is sick.

" Medicines ? Why not you give it to him ? " I asked him. He looked at me in fear.

" I.... I.... Think now you are his wife I think you should handle this " He said breaking his words.

How can he be so rude.

" But... " Before I speak.

" I am leaving mam " He said and bowed to me and walked out of the room. I looked at the medicines in my hand.

It's just medicines what a big deal about it.

I placed the medicines on table.

He will take it by himself.

Night 9:00pm

I made Ron sleep and walked to room.

I didn't seen him anywhere.

Servant dropped Ron to home.

" How was your day ? " Suddenly I heard a voice. As I turned around I seen Mike stood there.

He slowly started to walk towards me. He placed his hand on my cheek.

" Is Ron sleeping ? " He asked smiling at me. I nodded. He slowly placed a kiss on my forehead. We walked to his bedroom.

As we entered into the room. I seen the tablets on table.

" I forget to say you. Jack came here " I said and about to pick up the tablets.

" What did you just say ? " Suddenly he asked. I sensed a anger in his voice. He turned to me. I seen his eyes turned into red.

" J_ack.... " Before I say. He throwed his Brazer on ground angrily and came to me and pushed me to wall. Suddenly he placed his lips on my lips and started to kiss roughly.

He kissed me softly in morning. But now.... This kiss reminds me on last night.

" What.... Did you say ? " He asked breathing heavily.

" J_ack.... " I repeated. Suddenly he looked at me angrily. This time he gave a hard slap on my cheek. I placed my hand on cheek. Tears appeared in my eyes.

" HOW DARE YOU SAY ANOTHER MEN NAME ? " He yelled and hold my shoulders tightly. My eyes widen in shock seeing his anger.

" I... Am scared.... Please " I said crying badly.

" Kiss me " He said in frustration. I stood there numb. He ran his fingers on his hair.

" Kiss me " He said. Suddenly I seen a vibration on his body. He is shaking. He is not even looking at me.

" KISS ME !!! " This time he yelled looking into my eyes. I shivered and moved back.

" I.... Will kill myself. Come on !!! Kiss me " He said I seen tears in his eyes. I am just numb and looking at his body vibration. In a second he pulled a knife from the near table and placed it on his wrist.

" NO !!! " I yelled loudly in fear.

" Kiss me right now. I will kill myself. I am not joking " He said and pressed the knife on his wrist a little. I seen blood coming out of his body. Tears continuously flowing down my cheek.

I went to him and pressed my lips on his lips. I removed my lips.

" Throw it. Please.... " I requested in tears.

" This is not kiss " He said looking at me angrily.

" How did I kissed you last night ? Did you forget ? " He said angrily.

Last night started to repeat in my mind.

" If you don't kiss me Passionately. Before I kill myself. I am going to fuck you more worse than last night " He said angrily. My eyes widen in shock.

No.... No.... Last night. I can't bear it.

I used all my strength and started to kiss him passionately.

I started to kiss and kiss.

I don't know time. I keep on kissing him in tears.

" Don't call another men's name in front of me " He said calmly. He looked at me sadly and placed his hand on my cheek.

" I... Am sorry. I doesn't mean to hurt you " He said looking at my red cheek.

What kind of person he is ? Can't able to get him ?

" Let's sleep. I am so tired. Lots of work in office " He said and made me sleep on bed. I am shivering and sweating. I am about to get up.

" Where are you going ? " He asked quickly.

" I... I... Want to use washroom " I said in fear. He came closer to me and gave a small kiss on my lips.

" Be fast. I can't sleep when you aren't beside me " He said while smiling.

For God sake please don't smile.

I nodded and ran into the washroom. I locked it quickly and on all the taps and started to cry covering my mouth with my hand.

He scares me. He is monster. He is evil. He is dangerous.

If it's not for Ron. I wouldn't be staying here.

Past

" You gone Marry me. " He said angrily.

" No, I won't. Never " I said angrily and pushed him.

" GUARDS !!! " He yelled loudly. I seen 2-3 people's gathered around me. I turned to him.

" You don't have choice " He said while smiling.

" Dont you think about Ron future ? I mean about his school , His career, His needs. " He said looking at me.

" Do you know my brother ? You are following me ? " I said angrily.

" Sorry , Not following. It's called investigation " He said smiling at me. I stood there in tears.

" Why me ? " I asked sadly.

" Because I want only you " He said.

I have to think about Ron's future. Being like this I can't even give him a better future.

I can sacrifice myself for Ron.

" I will marry you " I said in one go.

....

" Exchange your rings " Preist said.

He invited lots of people within 24 hours.

Where is Ron ? He wont let me see Ron.

We started to exchange rings.

" You can kiss your bride " Priest said.

" Where is Ron ? " I whispered slowly. In a second he pulled me and kissed my forehead.

How can he kiss me ?

Past ends.

I opened my eyes slowly. I looked at watch.

Shut !!!

Ron is going to be late for school.

" Wifey " Suddenly I hear his sound. As I turned a side I seen him in towel. I walked to me and got on bed. I started to sweat.

" Good morning " He said while smiling and kissed my forehead. Suddenly my phone started to ring. He looked at the table which the phone is on it. He noticed the medicines beside my phone. I seen a anger in his face.

He pulled my wrist tightly.

" Where did you get this medicines ? " He asked looking at me angrily. Tears appeared in my eyes.

" Ja ..... Your assistant told me to give you " I said.

I can't face the consequences by telling his name again.

" Throw them out " He said angrily looking into my eyes. I gave a quick nod. I got out of the bed. I am literally shivering. I am about to take the medicines.

" Sis " Suddenly I heard Ron voice. I seen him in school uniform.

He must be waiting for me to drop in school.

" Ron " I called his name and ran to him and kneeled down and hugged him tightly.

I have only you. I can't let you see his anger and his monster inside him.

" Don't you drop me in school ? " He asked sadly. I quickly wiped my tears. I broke the hug and smiled.

" Of course. Let us drop you together " suddenly Mike said walking towards us. I hold Ron's hand tightly. I looked at Mike. His eyes are now so cool. He smiled looking at me.

....

After dropping Ron at school.

Now we both are in car. Mike is driving. While I sat on seat just like a ice with no movement. I am scared seating alone with him.

" Do you want to go somewhere ? Like Park, Restaurant.... " Before he complete.

" No " I rejected him. He looked at me surprised. Suddenly he took my hand. I got scared.

" What happened ? " He asked in confused while fixing his eyes on road.

" Nothing " I said and Exhaled my breath. Suddenly he stopped the car aside. Panic started in me. In a minute he took my face in his hands my eyes widen in shock.

" Why are you scared ? " He asked seriously looking into my eyes.

" I.... Am not " I said in shiver. He removed his hands from me. He hit the stir wheel hardly. I shivered a second.

" Why ? Why ? " Mike said in frustration.

What why ?

" Why Everyone gets scared of me ? " He asked sadly. I looked at him. I seen a sad face. He had tears in his eyes. I am about to place my hand on his shoulder.

No, Avery

He is a PYSCO.

He is a monster.

He is a devil.

He kills himself more than you.

" I love you " He said in tears looking into my eyes.

This isn't love Mike. I am expecting this love.

" I love you forever and ever " He said and pulled me into a tight hug.

" Don't be scared of me. Please " Mike requested. He started to cry.

Mike is crying ? I am mean why ?

He started to cry and cry in my arms. I didn't even hugged him. I am just shocked.

In a minute he becomes violent in a minute he becomes cool. What he is exactly ?

I can't forgive him for what he did on that night with me. It's just a bad nightmare to me.

It's already been a hour he is still in my arms.

Is he sleeping or something ?

" Mike ? " I called his name. There is no response. I tapped his back slowly.

" Mike ? " I called him again. Suddenly he is unconscious on my shoulder.

" MIKE !!! " I yelled loudly. I looked at his face. His eyes are closed.

....

" Did you called the doctor ? " I asked jack.

Right now we are in his house. He is on his bed laying unconscious.

" Yes, Madam " He said.

" Please get out " Suddenly I heard a voice. As we turned.

" Doctor stefen ? " Jack said.

Doctor stefen.

My eyes widen in shock hearing his name.

Is he the doctor stefen that sent me the letter on my wedding day ?

Past.

After all the marriage rituals are done.

I sat on the beach thinking about Ron.

I want to see him. I seen Mike talking to guests and his eyes is on me.

I am already in bad mood.

" No, I don't " I said and turned my face. Suddenly he throwed a piece of paper on my lap. Before I look at him he is gone. I looked at Mike he is busy in talking.

What is this ?

I slowly opened the paper. I made sure that Mike didn't see it.

" If you want to escape meet me upstairs at Villa

Doctor Stefen "

Who is it ? Who wants to help me ? I don't know anybody.

Who is doctor stefen.

I got up and about to go.

" where are you going ? " Suddenly I heard Mike voice. My heart skipped hearing his voice. I quickly hide the paper. I looked at him.

" I... Want to use washroom " I said while faking a smile. He looked at me from top to bottom.

" Washroom ? " He asked suspiciously. I gave nod.

" Let's go together " He said and pulled my waist. I started shivering. I hold the piece of paper tightly in my fist.

" Also the party is over. Let's get back to our home " He said while smiling. I gave a nod. I started sweating. Suddenly in a second he pulled the paper from my hand.

" No " I yelled. Mike looked into it. Suddenly I seen his eyes turned into red. He looked at me.

I started to shiver. I am about to escape. He pulled my wrist.

" GUARD !!! " He screamed looking at me. I seen a guard ran to us.

" Yes, Sir " he asked bowing his head.

" Tell everyone the party is over " He said and in a second he started to drag me.

He threw me in a car. Tears appeared in my eyes.

Where is he taking me ?

After an hour. He stopped in front of a huge villa. He came to me and dragged me out and took me inside the house.

I can't able to see anything other than a scare and a fear.

I just realized he dragged me into bedroom. He threw me on bed. He quickly locked the door.

No... No.... Don't do anything to me.

" I...." Before I speak. Suddenly i seen a monster in him. He looked at me. I moved back on bed.

I seen the bed is decorated with red roses.

Now I looked around the room which is fully decorated with flowers , candles.

He came on bed. He slowly placed his hand on my cheek.

" Don't you love me ? " He asked. I heard a vibration in his voice. I seen him smiling.

" No, I don't love you. Leave me " I said angrily in tears. He pulled my wrist.

" No, you love me " He said while smiling.

Is he crazy ?

" I DON'T " I yelled angrily.

" YOU LOVE ME " He screamed angrily. In a second he started to kiss me. I started to beat his back.

His kiss as more strength that I can't able to push him.

Suddenly he stopped.

" Don't you want Ron ? " He asked angrily. My eyes widen in shock.

" No, Please don't do anything to him. He is just a small kid " I said while crying.

" No... No... No... Don't cry " he said wiping my tears. I just crying there on bed.

" I am evil.... I am evil..... I made you cry. I have to die " He said and in a second he got out of the bed. In a second he started to hit his head on wall badly.

" Stop !! What are you doing ? " I yelled.

" You don't love me. I deserve to die " He said hitting on wall. Suddenly I seen his head bleeding. My eyes widen in shock. I got of the bed.

" I LOVE YOU " I yelled loudly in tears. In a second he stopped. He ran to me and hugged me tightly.

" I know you love me. I know. " He said and in a second he kissed me. Tears rolled down my cheek. In a second he started to kiss me more passionately.

I lifted me and placed me on bed. He started to kiss every part on mine.

He slowly kissed my ear. Tears rolled in my eyes. He lifted me up and pulled my shirt off. His eyes are rolling around my body. He turned me back. He placed his hand on my bra hook.

" You belong to me " he whispered in my ear.

I am shivering. In a second he removed my bra. I started to cover myself. He made me lay on bed. And got on top of me. He quickly remove his shirt and pants.

In a second he inserted his xxx into me.

" Ah.... " I yelled in pain and opened my teary eyes.

" Is it paining ? " He asked in worried tone. I started to cry badly.

This is the only time I can cry openly.

" Shh.... It's going to be fine. Look at me " He said holding my face. I just keep on crying and crying.

" Ok.. ok... I will stop " He said and removed from me. I am just a died person there.

Lifeless.... You are a PYSCO

He looked at me crying and pulled me into a tight hug.

" I... I promise I won't do it again. Please don't cry " He said in tears and hugged me tightly.

I keep on crying the whole night.

I didn't care where I am. I didn't care PYSCO Mike is beside me. I just keep on crying.

This night had been a bad nightmare.

" Don't cry , please " Mike said. I didn't care about him. He hugged me so tightly.

That's the end of the chapter. if you like please vote, comment share the story.

PYSCO

A very point of view

    Dr. Stefen.

" Please go out. I want to check him " Stefen said. Me and jack nodded and got out of the room.

Is he the same person I have been looking for ?

Dr. Stefen is the name which I received the letter from.

He as a secret of Mike. I have to ask him.

After a few minutes I seen him came out of the room.

" Is he okay ? " I asked. He walked to me.

" He is not taking his medicines " Stefen said in sad tone.

Medicines ?

Yes, jack gave me last night.

" Is he serious ? " I asked in concerned.

" Of course he is, Being his wife don't you think you should take care of him ? " He said a little rude. I looked at him in confused.

" I... " Before I speak.

" He is my friend. I can't see my friend like this " He said in sad tone.

" Do you know how he cares about you ? He loves you more than anyone in this world. He sacrifice his life if you just say a word " He started to yell at me.

That's enough he can't yell at me. He don't know about his PYSCO behavior.

" LOVE ? Do you call love Dr. Stefen ? Do you even know how he behaves ? He... " Before I complete.

" Do you want to know what exactly is Mike ? " He said angrily and in a second he pulled my hand and took me into our bedroom.

" What are you doing Dr. Stefen ? " I said angrily and shook off my hand. He went to Mike who is on bed sleeping and pulled out a key from his pocket. He went to the closet.

What he is doing ?

He opened the locker and pulled out a book from it. He throwed the book in front of me angrily.

" Read it. You will get to know what he is actually " He said angrily. I looked at him in confused. He came to me and looked into my eyes.

" He is not like you see. Don't forget to give him medicines. It's important. I am sure you can handle him. " He said in soft tone. He walked to the door.

" I am Happy that you didn't came looking for me that day " He said. I turned to him Without even looking back he walked off.

So he is the same person who sent me the letter.

The person who tried to help me now he is supporting Mike.

I picked up the book. I gave a look at Mike who is in deep sleep.

What this book contain ?

I sat on chair and slowly opened the page.

MR. WILSON MIKE.

Written on the middle of the page. I turned to another page.

20 September 1990.

" Why ? Why ? I deserve happiness.

Why my parents keep on fighting daily ? I can't able to hear there screaming. I locked myself inside the bathroom and turned on all the taps and closed my ears tightly.

Please stop !!!

Stop fighting it's hurting me.

I just want a happy family. I don't want my parents to fight daily.

Suddenly I heard a scream from downstairs. I ran downstairs only to found my mother died there.

There is blood all over the floor. Mother is filled with blood all over her body. I seen dad hold the knife in his hand.

I ran to mom and started to cry. The anger filled in me. I went to dad and pulled his collar.

" I am gone kill you "

I pulled a vase and I hit on his head so hard. He died in a spot. I quickly throwed the vase.

I killed a person. I killed my father.

No... No.... I am not a murderer. "

I flipped to another page.

1 December 1994

" I became a top billionaire around a world. I worked so hard so hard. I gained everything power, Money, Status, respect. Everything..... But...

After a few months I realized myself that I am becoming a monster.

I always been in a vibration. I am not man I use to be. I started to lock myself in a room. I started to draw a different types of horror pictures. "

I seen a picture he draw.

The picture is about a man killing a women there is blood, evil, monster in a man's eyes.

The picture is just so scary.

I started to sweat. I am literally shaking seeing the picture.

" W_ater " suddenly I heard a voice. I gasped and seen that Mike is about to wake up. I quickly place the picture into the diary and quickly hide it in my closet. I ran to closet and closed the locker.

I have to find more in it.

I went to Mike and stood in front of him like nothing happened.

" W_ater " He whispered slowly and got seated on bed. I quickly pour the glass of water and gave it to him. He took a sip of water and looked at me.

" What happened ? " He asked looking at me.

" Nothing " I said and about to turn around. In a second he pulled my wrist. I fell on bed. We are so close together. I looked into his eyes. His eyes are dull and lifeless.

" Who treated me ? " He asked in slow tone.

" Dr..... " I stopped.

No, I can't call his name. He will torture me again.

" Dr ? " He asked.

" I... I... Mean doctor treated you " I said in scared. He chuckled.

" Does the doctor as no name ? " He asked while laughing.

He is laughing. Mike is laughing. He is even asking the name of the men.

" Dr.... Dr..... " I am scared to say the name. He rubbed his finger on my cheek.

" What ? " He asked in confused.

He don't know what he did ?

He don't like when I call men's name.

" Dr. Stefen " I said in one go and closed my eyes tightly.

Now he will kill me. I am sure.

" Stefen ? That crazy man is still Being my doctor. " He said in soft tone. I opened my eyes slowly. He is just so cool and relaxed and not being angry at me. I am just started to stare at him.

" Did something happened ? Where is Ron ? I didn't seen him from the day of our marriage " He asked looking around.

What's happening to him ? Why don't he remember anything ? What did Dr. Stefen do to him ?

He remembers our marriage but not Ron ?

I have to call Dr. Stefen.

" Avery ? " I heard he called my name.

He called my name. It's first time he called my name.

" Are you okay ? You look distracted " He asked.

" No... No... I am fine. Ron went to school. " I said. He looked at me.

What's happening here ? I have to ask Dr. Stefen right now.

" You might be hungry. I will bring something to eat " I said.

" Hmm " He nodded. I walked out of the room.

What's happening to him ? Where is Dr. Stefen ? How can I find him ?

Jack. Yes, jack knows where is he.

I quickly called jack and took his number.

I dialed to Dr. Stefen.

" I know you will call " He said in calm voice.

" What happened to him ? He is completely different. He don't remember a single thing he had done to me. " I said in angry tone.

" Did you gave him medicines ? " He asked.

" I am asking you how he changed. You damn caring about medicines " I yelled angrily.

" Cool Avery. "

" You know my name. What is happening here ? " I asked in shock.

" He is not completely cured Avery. He still has the PYSCO in him. You will be the cure to him. Just Ask him to take the medicines " He said.

" You know.... You know right he is PYSCO. Still you are not helping me and backing off now. On our wedding day you are the one right who willing to help me. Then what happened that you are not helping me now and letting me live with this PYSCO ? "

I started to ask him questions.

" I know. I tried to save you that day. But.... But... I think it's not right. Mike will change Avery. He will change when you are beside him. " He said in sad tone.

" I mean... Are you insane ? How can I change a PYSCO ? Who is so obsessed with me. He... He... Scares me. I am literally scared of him. How can you think that I can save him ? " I said angrily.

" A person who killed his own father it's just a small thing to kill me and Ron. Do you get that ? " I said angrily.

" I think you just read his dairy a little. I think you should read more to get to know him. "

I placed my hand on my head.

That's enough. This conversation is making me angry.

Screw that damn dairy.

" Just give him medicines " He said.

" Medicines ? I am asking help from you and you are telling me to take care of your dearest friend " I said angrily.

" Listen Avery. Just give him medicines and see how he reacts. Then you will get to know his dark side " He said seriously.

Medicines ? How is this all related to medicines ?

I have to give it a try.

I hung up the call. I slowly walked into the bedroom. I seen him on bed reading a book. He looked at me.

" Is it done ? " He asked while smiling.

" Huh ? "

I keep on thinking where did I kept this medicines ?

My eyes landed on the table. It's on table.

" I mean food. I am hungry " He asked. I started to sweat.

What exactly Dr. Stefen mean ?

I have to find him.

I don't care how mister he is. Today I have to find it and let go out of his life.

" Before eating I think you have to take something " I said. I slowly walked towards the table and picked up the tablets. He looked at the tablets.

Suddenly the smile on his face faded off. I seen a different expression of his face.

He started to look another side.

" Medicines " I said taking to him. He not even looking at me.

" I don't need it " He said. I seen a vibration in his voice. He is shivering and sweating.

" You have to take it. " I said and pulled a pill.

" I said I won't take it " This time he said a little angrily. I walked to him and placed the tablet in front of his mouth.

" I DON'T WANT IT ". He yelled angrily and throwed the pill on ground angrily. He looked at me angrily his eyes are full of red.

Avery what have you done ?

He looks different now.

He pulled my arm tightly.

" When I said don't. Then don't " He said angrily looking into my eyes. I am scared looking at him.

He looks like a monster. A tear rolled in my eyes.

" Do you understand ? " He asked while smiling. I am just sobbing there in fear.

" DO YOU UNDERSTAND ? " He yelled this time. I gave a quick nod. I started to cry. Suddenly I seen that he released my arm.

" What did I do ? " Suddenly Mike asked in sad tone looking at me. He about to place his hand on my face. I shivered in tears.

" I did something " He said. I keep on crying and shivering there.

" Avery.... I.... " He whispered. In a second he pulled me into a tight hug. I am shivering in his arms.

" I... Won't harm you. I.... Am sorry " He said.

" Don't cry " He said. Suddenly I felt unconscious.

" Avery.... Avery " I started to hear his voice.

" AVERY !!! "

....

As I opened my eyes. I seen my myself on bed. I got up slowly.

This head is killing me.

I looked around i didn't seen Mike anywhere.

Where is he ? Did he do something to Ron ?

I ran out of the room. I started to search every corner. But he is no where. I walked out of the house.

There I seen him in garden. He is crying like anything.

He is crying ?

I walked to him slowly. I got down.

" Mike ? " I called him.

" Please.... Don't get near me. I am a monster " He said while crying.

What he is saying ?

" I am a PYSCO Avery " he said looking into my eyes.

Suddenly a pain hit in my heart.

" You..... are not " I said controlling my tears.

" I am Avery " He said in tears.

" Day by day I am scaring you. I am making you shiver. I am an idiot that I am damn saying that I am loving you " He said while crying. Tears rolled in my eyes.

Why am I crying ? I have no feeling for him ?

" No " I said while crying

In a second I pulled him to my chest.

Hey guys for a long time. Hope you guys like it.

I am scared

A very point of view

It's been two days.

Ron is sleeping beside me. I looked at his cute little face and a tear rolled down my cheek.

Why we were stucked in this house Ron ? We use to be so happy together without any luxurious. I made all this. I made my life a hell and agreed to this marriage.

Whatever the reason may be still....

My husband is a PYSCO.

How can I cure him ? When I am scared of him.

" Is he sleeping ? " Suddenly I heard his rough voice. I looked at Mike who is leaning on the door.

" Y_es " I whispered slowly. I pulled the blanket and covered Ron. I gave a small kiss on his forehead.

" Do you want to sleep here with Ron ? " He asked coming towards the bed.

I started shivering. He killed his father. Killing me and Ron is just so simple to him.

I gave a quick nod.

" Let's sleep together " He said.

Together ?

He walked to me and kissed my forehead.

He again forget about what happened 2 days back. I have to call Dr. Stefen. I have to ask what happening to Mike exactly.

After a few minutes. I seen him coming into the room. He wore his night clothes. I acted like I am in deep sleep. I sensed his lips on mine. He removed my hair locks behind my ear.

After a few minutes I didn't sensed any of his touch. I opened my eyes slowly. There I seen him taking off the shirt looking at the mirror.

Tattoos..... His 6 pack body as tattoos all over.

Evey tattoo has something. What it define ? Why he as scary tattoos on his body ?

I read the diary half. I have to read more.

" Sis " suddenly I heard Ron whisper. I closed my eyes tightly.

" Sis " This time. I heard Ron crying. I opened my eyes quickly. I seen Mike ran to the bed. I looked at Ron crying closing his eyes tightly.

" Ron, wake up. Look it's sister. You are dreaming " I said taking him Into my arms and hugged him tightly.

" What happened ? " Mike asked in concerned. As he sat beside me. He placed his hand on Ron's head.

" He is just dreaming. It's routine " I said tapping Ron's back. Mike nodded. Suddenly I seen Mike started to think something.

" What happened ? " I asked Mike. He came out of his thoughts.

" I too get bad nightmares. But.... But... " Mike started to say but stopped. He got off the bed. I placed the Ron on bed. I looked at Mike who went to the balcony.

What happened to him ?

I went to balcony. I seen Mike stood there looking at the sky. I walked to him and stood beside him.

" My mom use to say sharing sorrows makes you better " I said looking at the sky. In a second I seen him pulled me into his arms tightly.

I got shocked by his move.

" Let me hug you for a minute " He said. I sensed his voice. His voice is so low and sad. I started to look at the tattoo on his chest.

" Please don't hate me "

" Avery is scared of me "

" I want to make Avery happy "

" Avery.... " Before I read. Mike broke the hug.

80% tattoos on his body as my name on it.

What kind of love is this ?

" Go and sleep " Mike said. My eyes are on his body. Tear rolled in my eyes. I am about to touch his tattoos. Mike hold my hand quickly. I looked at him he nodded as no sadly.

" Why ? Why your body is full of my name ? " I asked sadly. He is about to go. I came in front of him.

" Today you have to say your secrets. If not... I am going to leave you " I said in tears. Suddenly Mike pulled my wrist.

" DON'T YOU DARE !!! " Mike shouted angrily. I got scared.

No... If he kills me let him do it. I will get to know his secrets today.

" Do not kill anyone. " I seen the tattoo.

" What does it mean Mike ? Why you have this scary tattoos on your body ? " I pulled myself and hold my fist tightly. I am scared from inside but gathered all my strength together to ask him.

He ignored me and walked inside the bedroom. I followed him. He quickly wore his shirt. I walked to him.

" You don't want me to see your tattoos right ? " I asked him. In a second he turned to me and looked at me angrily.

" You want to know my secrets right ? you want to see my real face right ? Today I will show want is Mike Wilson " He said angrily. In a second he pulled my hand and took me out of the room.

He is holding my hand tightly. It's paining.

He dragged me into the lift and pressed the top floor button.

From the day of my marrige. I didn't seen his house. I always use to stay at 5th floor.

The minute we reached top floor. He pulled me out and walked towards a room. He quickly typed a passcode the door opened. He pushed me into the room. I fell on the ground. The room is so dark. I can't able to see anything.

Suddenly he switched on the lights. I barely opened my eyes slowly. I placed my hand in front of my eyes to cover from the light.

After I got adjusted to the light. I explored around. The minute I seen around. My eyes widen in shock.

I seen a scary paintings on the wall. There is blood in every painting. I seen different kinds of knifes , blades , etc.... All harmful objects.

I started to shiver. Suddenly Mike came to me and pulled me up. I got scared when he touched me.

" Come " He said and pulled my hand and made me stood in front of a scary picture.

" Look.... Look.... Look carefully. This all the pictures I had painted. Do you know what it means ? " He asked making me stare at the scary picture. I started to shiver and almost out of breath. Tears continuously rolling down my cheek. He made me look into his eyes.

" It means i am a PYSCO " He shouted angrily.

" Don't you know what PYSCO do ? I will tell you today " He said angrily. In a second he removed his shirt. Suddenly he pulled out a machine.

It's tattoo machine.

He pulled me and made me sit on a chair forcely. He took a seat in front of me.

" What tattoo should I do today ? " He asked looking at me. My eyes widen in shock.

Is he going to make tatoo in front of me ?

" Tell me Avery. What tattoo do you like ? How about I draw your face on my chest ? "

No.... No.... It hurts....

" Let me start " He said and about to start. I closed my eyes tightly in fear. Suddenly he hold my hand. I shivered and opened my eyes quickly.

" I have lots of tattoos Avery. Look here your name. Here your favorite food. Here.... " He said showing me his tattoos on his body.

" I have your name all over my body. How about I write my name on your body ? " He said while smiling. My eyes widen in shock.

No.... No.... It pains. I don't want any tattoos.

" NO !!!! " I screamed while sobbing. He took my face in his hands.

" It's just a few minutes. It won't pain. " He said looking into my eyes.

" Why..... Are you doing this to me ? " I asked in tears.

" We are married Avery. Nobody can take you from me. I will mark you with my name. You belong to me " He said while smiling.

" Mike..... I.... Am scared.... Please stop it " I begged him. He slowly wiped my tears.

" It's just a few minutes " He said.

" I will mark my name in a place that nobody will see my name on your body " He said.

" How about on stomach ? No... No.... When you give birth to my child they will cut your stomach. No... No.... Then.... How about on your waist ? " He said.

My eyes widen in shock. I am literally shaking. I am trying to escape. He hold my hands so tightly that I can't able to move.

In a second he removed my shirt.

" Mike... No... " Before I beg. He lifted me in his arms and made me lay on the bed. He had the machine in his hand. He quickly got on top of me.

" No... Please... " I started to cry. In a second he pressed the needle into my waist.

" AH.... " I yelled in pain struggling here and there.

" It's done.... Almost done Avery " He said. I seen blood coming out of my body. I started to yell in pain.

After a few minutes.

The tattoo is done. I am just lifeless laying on bed. I now don't even have a strength to even fight back. The minute he done tattoo. He bent down and gave a small kiss on the tattoo. A pain hit me.

He looked at me and hugged me tightly.

He broke the hug. He pulled my shirt and made me wear it. I am so scared of him. My eyes were completely filled with tears.

Mike pulled me closer to him.

" I love you. I love you so much than anyone in this world. I never loved anyone more than you " He said looking into my eyes.

This is not love.

" Do you love childern ? " He asked quickly.

I am in so shock that I don't have any strength to listen to his words.

I didn't replied and remained silent.

" Ofcourse you love. I seen you taking care of Ron as your own child. " He said pulling me closer to him. I am literally so scared of him. He looks cool now but...

" I am sleepy " He said yawning and quickly pulled me more closer. Our faces are so close together.

I am scared of you.

After a few minutes I too felt sleepy and closed my eyes.

Mike point of view

I opened my eyes slowly. I found myself on the lap.

I looked at Avery she is sleeping soundly.

Did i do something Last night ? I woke up quickly. I looked around. My eyes widen in shock seeing the room.

Why did I bring her here ?

Did she came to know that I am mentally unstable ?

What exactly happened ? I can't able to remember anything.

The last things I remember is that. I met Avery in hotel. We married. But.... Why can't I remember that did we married happily ? I met Avery brother Ron. I joined him in school.

The last time I am on bed Avery spoke to me about my doctor.

Then.... That's right I hugged Avery and cried and told that I am PYSCO and told her to be far away from me.

Then why did I brought her here ? She must be scared knowing about my behavior.

A tear rolled down my cheek.

I quickly took Avery into my arms.

....

I made her lay on our bed. I covered her with blanket.

What i am doing exactly with this poor girl ?

I have to call Dr. Stefen.

I quickly pulled out my phone.

" Stefen ? " I called his name.

" Are you not taking your medicines again Mike ? " He asked in cool tone.

" Stefen listen to me. I had done something to Avery I can't able to remember. My health is on stable right ? You said right I am stable now and not doing any unpleasant things. Then.... Why I ended up in that room with Avery ? " I asked in worried tone.

" What ? You.... You... Took her to that terrible room. You know right what it means ? " Stefen said angrily.

" But.... You said I am cured then why am I still doing those PYSCO things again ? Am I not cured stefen ? " I asked. There is a silence on other side.

" STEFEN !!! " I yelled angrily.

" Mike.... You... Are not completely cured. It's... " Before he speak.

It means I am... I am... Still that PYSCO Mike. I.... Married her and making her scare daily.

I am in PYSCO all this days.

I am literally shocked. I should've guessed when he started to ask me to take medicines all this time.

" Mike ? Mike ? Are you there ? I will be coming to your home. Let's talk " Stefen said. I ignored him. I quickly hung up the call.

What I have been doing to this poor girl and Ron ?

I started to cry tears continuously flowing down my cheek.

Why didn't you escaped avery ? Why did you stayed with a beast like me ? You don't know me.

" Ah... " Suddenly I heard Avery woke up slowly. I quickly wiped my tears and ran to her. I sat beside her. The minute she seen me. She got scared and moved back.

" No.... Please don't.... " She said while crying and shivering. A pain hit in my heart seeing her crying.

" Avery , listen to me " I said and about to touch her. She looked at me in fear. She pulled herself closer. I am about to pull her into a hug. She pushed my hand. I got slipped for support I quickly grabbed her waist.

" AH.... " She yelled in pain. I looked at her in confused.

" What happened ? " I asked in worried tone looking at her waist. She started to move away from me. I pulled her quickly and lifted her shirt.

That's all. I got numb. My eyes widen in shock. Tears rolled in my eyes. I seen my name of tattoo on her waist.

Did I do it ? I done that. She must be scared. It must be hurting her.

I got up from bed slowly. She covered herself with blanket quickly.

" Uncle " Suddenly I heard a cute little voice. As I turned around. I seen Ron. He ran to me and hugged my legs. In a second I seen Avery came to ron and pulled him away from me. And lifted him in his arms.

" Sis, What happened ? Why are you not letting me to hug uncle ? " He asked softly.

" Ron... Let's... Leave from here " She said in fear. And ran towards the door.

You can't leave me.

In a second I stood in front of her.

" You.... Can't leave me " I said. She started to take steps back holding Ron tightly.

" please.... Let us go " she said while crying. I slowly placed my hand on Ron's head.

" JACK !!! " I shouted loudly. I seen jack came running into the room.

" Take Ron to his room. " I said angrily staring at Avery.

" No... No... " Avery said and pulled Ron to him closer. Jack went to him.

" I want to stay with sis " Ron said.

" DONT YOU GET IT ? " I yelled angrily. In a second he pulled Ron from Avery.

" Sis.... Sis " Ron started to cry.

" RON !!! " Avery yelled loudly while crying.

" Ron , There are lots of chocolates in your room. Go get them. I am going to talk to your sister " I said while smiling.

" Really ? " Ron asked and stopped crying. I gave a nod. Jack took Ron with him. Avery is about to go.

" RON " I pulled her to me.

" Please.... Let us go " she asked while crying.

" I love you Avery. Please don't leave me " I said in sad tone wiping her tears.

" ITS NOT LOVE YOU ARE A PYSCO " She yelled angrily. A pain hit in my heart. I quickly released her. In a second I seen she ran out of the room. I stood there in tears.

You are right I am PYSCO.

I stood there crying silently.

Don't leave me Avery.

" MAM " suddenly I heard a scream. As I ran out of the room. I heard the sound from the swimming pool area.

As I got there. I shocked to see Avery jumped into the pool and guard rescued her.

I ran to her and hold her. She coughed all the water out.

" Avery... Avery " I started to call her name. She slowly opened her eyes. The minute she seen me she pushed me and got up and about to ran.

" BLANKET " I screamed at guard. He gave me the blanket. I pulled it and ran behind Avery and caught her and covered her with blanket.

" Please.... Listen to me " I requested while crying.

" Leave me. I am scared of you. " She said in fear. I pulled her tightly.

" Avery.... Once listen to me. I know. I know what you feel. But.... " Before I speak. She looked at me in tears.

" Do you know how the tattoo hurts ? " She asked in tears. In a second she collapsed In my arms.

" AVERY " I yelled.

Sorry guys for the late update. Actually I'm busy in writing other books.

Please do vote, share, comment.

I hope you like this update.

His truth

A very point of view

I opened my eyes slowly. I seen myself in my bedroom. I am weak. My body aches every where. I slowly got seated and leaned on pillow.

I seen my wrist is injected.

What happened to me ?

" You shouldn't get up " Suddenly I heard a voice. As I turned to that direction.

" Dr.... Stefen " I called his name slowly. I am so damn weak. He walked to me and got seated on chair in front of me.

" You might be having a lots of questions regarding Mike.

Come on !!

Shoot them " He asked while giving his bright smile.

Now I don't have any questions. I am done with him. I am going to leave him. After what happened last night it's just....

" Avery ? " I came out of my thoughts.

" Look.... I don't have strength to talk with you. I don't want...to leave with him. " I just said that and my eyes started to close slowly.

Why I'm so weak ?

" You have heavy fever. It's better if you rest for few more days " He said. I giggled.

" Rest ? " I smiled.

" Don't you want to see Ron ? " He asked softly.

Yes, where is Ron ? Did Mike do something to him ?

I quickly straighten my body.

" Where is Ron ? Is he okay ? Mike didn't killed him right ? " I asked in worried tone. A small tears filled in my eyes.

" He is not a murderer " Stefen said in a little anger voice.

" A man who killed his father. What do you call it Dr. Stefen ? " I said angrily looking at him.

" Do you know what Mike is doing right now ? " He asked angrily and stood up quickly.

How would I know.

" He is punishing himself for torturing you last night. He went into the same room. And from past 3 hours he didn't came outside. Do you get that Avery ? " He said angrily.

" I asked you about my brother not him. " I said angrily. He stood there looking at me angrily. He is not going to answer me.

Fine. I will find Ron myself.

I am about to remove the injection.

" Stop it !!! He is with jack " stefen said. I let out a breath.

My god he is fine.

" Where is the dairy ? " He asked.

What's with that stupid dairy ?

" It's in his locker " I said and turned my face.

He is just supporting his PYSCO friend.

Stefen went to closet and pulled out the dairy. He came to me.

" Read it completely " He said giving me the dairy. I throwed the dairy angrily it got landed on floor.

" AVERY !!! " Stefen yelled angrily.

" It's hell living here. I am fed up acting in front of him. Now I don't want this marriage and I don't want this stupid ring in my hand " I said angrily tears rolled down my cheek. In a second I pulled the ring and throwed on ground.

" Fine. Fine. I will show you something " Stefen said controlling his anger. He pulled the phone from his pocket. He throwed the mobile on me.

" Look it. Come on look it. " He said. I picked up the phone slowly. I pressed the play button.

My eyes widen when I seen what's in there.

I seen Mike is in the same room where he took me last night.

He started Making tattoos on his body again. Blood is all over his body.

I closed my eyes tightly.

" Look. I told you he is PYSCO. " I said angrily.

" Yes, He is PYSCO. But do you know what ? He never been to that room ever since he married you. He came to me and begged me to cure him when he first got to know his behaviour. I tried using everything to cure him. But.... But.... It didn't worked. His behaviour is getting more and more intense. I came to know that he is not taking his medicines. But....after a few months he told me that he is going to marry. " Stefen said in sad tone. I seen tears in his eyes.

Past.

" Mike, listen to me it's not the time for you to get married. you are still in treatment. I can't take this risk and let you suffer a innocent girl " I said in frustration.

" Stefen. When I first seen her. I got to know that she is the one who can cure me. She is the one who can let me out of this dark. I can feel her. I love her stefen. I love her " Mike said in sad tone.

" Look Mike. I know. But... You are still not cured. You don't know how you behave. You can't remember what you did. It's risky for you to get married. She will be in trouble. You will regret later " Stefen said.

" No, She is the key to my happy life. I can't lose her. I will never gone hurt her. If I do then I will punish myself " Mike said.

Avery point of view

The things he keeps on saying. I just got numb and tears are rolling down my cheek.

" On your wedding day after seeing you. I got to know that yes, only you can cure him. I told to him that he is cured. He is fine. He don't know anything he did to you. He only remember that he married you happily and he is making you happy. " Stefen said in tears. My eyes widen in shock.

He took the book and the ring from the ground. He walked to me and placed it on bed.

" Now it's your choice. Either you wear the ring or not. Read his dairy. " Stefen said. In a second he walked out of the room. I looked at the dairy and the ring.

I slowly picked up the dairy. I opened to tha page where I stopped.

December - 1991

I started to behave strangely. I can't able to understand my behavior. My employees, My workers started to be scared when they see me.

I started to lock myself in a room and started to draw the pictures of different scary monsters.

Soon I started to become a monster. I can't able to remember anything. Why it's happening to me ? Why ? Why ?

I started to punish myself. To remember myself I started to make tattoos on my body.

Every tattoo on my body as always been my one and only strength. When I see them I got to know what I am.

After a few months of suffering. I met a friend stefen. Most people got scared of me. I don't have friends, family nobody in my life.

Stefen has always been my soul friend. He is doctor. He started to treat me. But.... But.... My behavior started to be out of extent. Stefen seen it.

" Mike, You need a friend. A family. A support so that you can be cured " Stefen said.

" No.... No... I don't need anybody. I will kill them if they will be close to me "

" Mike, You didn't killed your father on purpose there is a reason behind it. Just come out of it. "

I started to feel pain. I use to go to th le same room and be there for days to get out my physco.

Medicines as became a poison to me. I get scared when I see them.

I started to get scary nightmares. Like I am killing someone.

Days, months, years as passed.

Finally I thought of sleeping with women. This is the only way for me to kill my inside PYSCO.

I started to search every women. Bold, most sexy, Best prostitutes. But I never found a women who I would lean on.

September - 1998

Finally a day as come. I seen a beautiful women in a hotel. She is just so beautiful. Her eyes. Her lips. That's all this the women I want to live with.

October :

My doctor said that I am cured. I am so happy finally the PYSCO in me is killed.

Her name is Avery. Avery and I married happily. Avery have a little brother. His name is Ron. Finally I have a family. I have a life. I will give you so much love Avery.

I turned to another page.

Today I hurt Avery. She cried and cried. No, I won't do it again. Whatever hurts her I am never going to do it never. I am never going to do with her on bed.

I flipped to another page. It's found empty.

That's the end.

Tears started to flow down my cheek. He is suffering all this time and I treated him badly. He said I am cure to him.

I am sorry Mike. I am sorry. From now on I am going to do anything to bring you back like you use to be.

If I am your cure then I am going to give myself to you completely.

I started to cry and cry.

....

" You are fine now. Just take the medicines I prescribed " Stefen said and removed the injection. I nodded.

" I want to see Mike " I said. Stefen looked at me shockingly.

" No way. He is now monster in his room. He will be dangerous right now. He will be fine when he is out of that room. " Stefen said.

" But... We can't leave him like that. I will save him " I said in sad tone.

" I appreciate Avery. But.... It's too dangerous for you to get into the room. He will be out of control. Although he locked the room from inside. " Stefen said.

" You said right I am cure to him. Then I will " I said.

" But.... It's dangerous Avery " stefen said angrily.

" I will handle him " I said confidentiality.

....

Stefen warned me to don't go. Still I stood in front of the same room. My hands are shaking. I'm sweating almost. I hold the key tightly in my hand. I placed the key and it opened quickly. My heart started to beat fastly.

I can do it. I can help him.

I opened the door slowly. There I seen him on ground with blood all over his body. I seen him lifeless. Tears rolled in my eyes. I ran to him.

" Mike " I called him and placed my hand on him. In a second he grabbed my wrist. I got scared. His angry eyes.

" What are you doing here ? " He asked angrily.

" I... I.... " I can't even able to speak in front of him. Tears rolling down my cheek. I am shivering.

" GET OUT !!! " He yelled loudly. My heart skipped a bit. I moved back.

" Let's... Get.... Bandage... On your wounds " I spoke while shaking. He came to me and pulled me up angrily.

" Kiss me " He said angrily. My eyes widen in shock. I seen his face every inch on his body covered with blood. In a second He pulled my lips. He started to kiss me hardly. His blood is getting into my mouth.

The kiss sounds are all over the room.

You can get through this Avery.

I slowly placed my hand on his face and moved my first step.

I closed my eyes. Tears dropped down my cheek.

Suddenly I felt Mike stopped kissing. I opened my eyes and looked at him. He looked at me in confused. He started breathing heavily. I looked at my lips. He wiped something on my lips.

It's blood.

" Do you love me ? " He asked in sad tone holding me tightly. I looked at him.

" Let me bandage your wounds " I said.

" Do you love me ? " He asked again I'm sad tone.

" Mike.... " Before I speak.

" Do you love me ? " He asked again on my lips.

" Let's fight this together " I said in sad tone. Tears rolling down my cheek.

" Do you love me ? " He asked again. He licked my tears. I closed my eyes. Suddenly I felt his hand slowly moving into my shirt. I felt his cold hand touching my stomach. I felt weird. I stopped his hand from moving. Mike looked at me. Suddenly he grabbed my wrist.

In a second he got to know.

" Where is the wedding ring ? " He asked angrily looking at my fingers.

It's on the table. I throwed it a few minutes back.

Suddenly Mike slapped me hardly on my cheek. I got collapsed on floor. I placed my hand on my cheek.

That's all I can't able to stop crying. In a second Mike kneeled in front of me.

" I am sorry..... I am sorry " Mike said while crying.

Mike point of view

I had something again. What did I do ? Why did I slapped her ?

I am on bed. Avery started to clean my wounds. I am just staring at her.

Tears are both in our eyes. While cleaning she started to look at my every tattoo.

After cleaning she made me wear my shirt.

" Did.... I do something again Avery ? Why did I slapped you ? " I asked controlling my tears. I took her hand. She didn't responded. I seen the red mark ok her cheek. I placed my finger on her cheek slowly.

" Ah... " She whispered in pain. I gasped. She ignored me and took a bowl from the tray and placed the spoon in front of me.

I ate it. She is not talking to me nor looking at me. Suddenly she pulled a medicine.

That's all I started to sweat. I am shaking. I turned my head.

" Mike ? " She called me. She took my face in her hands and made me look into her eyes.

" Just close your eyes " She said and gave a small smile.

Her smile is so beautiful. I done what she said.

" Open your mouth " She said. I got confused and opened my mouth a little. Suddenly I felt her lips inside my mouth. I opened my eyes quickly. I felt something got into my throat and i swallowed it. She removed from me.

" Drink some water " she just said that. And about to go. I stood up quickly and took her hand and made her face me.

" Avery.... " Before I speak. Avery took my hand and placed it on her heart.

" You said you love me right ? Are you going to listen to me from now on ? I will cure you. I will be your cure " She said. Tears rolled in my eyes.

" From now on I am your best friend. Will you be my friend Mike ? " She asked softly.

I always been in dark for years. I never been so close to anybody except stefen.

After years somebody asked me to be a friend. I smiled and let out a cry and pulled Avery into a tight hug.

" I will " I said hugging her tightly. I felt her hands around me. It's felt like a days when somebody hugs me. I felt her warm.

That's the end....

Thank you guys for the love and support.

I seen two people who voted for my book. I can't remember there names. But... Thank you so much for your votes. I am so happy. But... Do please comment me so that I know how you guys feel about my book.

Let's go out.

Mike point of view

As I woke up. I didn't seen Avery anywhere.

So, she slept in Ron's room again.

I don't deserve her. I can't even tell her to sleep beside me when I did so terrible things to her.

The injuries on my body still not yet healed.

Tears rolled in my eyes. I got up slowly and about to get inside the washroom.

" Uncle " Suddenly I heard a sute little voice. The minute I turned. I seen Ron came running to me and hugged my legs tightly. A smiled appeared on my face. I lifted him slowly in my arms.

" My little pumpkin " I said and kissed his cheeks.

" Pumpkin ? Is it my nick name uncle ? " Ron asked in excitement.

I can't remember what I use to call him. But.... From today on I will call him pumpkin

" Yes "

" Hurry !!!! " Pumpkin clapped with his little hands.

" Where is your sister ? " I asked quickly.

I want to know is she ok after what happened yesterday.

" Sis preparing breakfast. She told me to call you " Pumpkin said with his cute little voice.

Breakfast. I tasted her food one time it's so delicious.

" You go down. Let uncle get freshed up " I said while smiling. Ron nodded and I placed him down. He ran outside with his little legs.

After I got a hot shower I got down. There I seen Avery in kitchen. She is wearing her night pants. Her hair is wrapped into a bun. Small hair locks are falling on her face.

While ron is seated on kitchen platform both look so adorable. I walked into the kitchen.

The minute I entered into the kitchen. The smile I seen on her face faded off. Our eyes met.

" Uncle " pumpkin opened his arms. I diverted my attention to ron. I pulled him into my arms.

" Uncle. We are going out " Pumpkin said in excitement. I looked at Avery in confused.

" Ron what's to visit the amusement park. He loves it. I use to take him on every Sunday.... But... After I came here I didn't got a enough time to spend with him " Avery said while placed a small smile on her face. I gave a nod.

" I will arrange the body guard's. You can take my car.... " Before I speak completely.

" You are coming with us " Avery ordered. I looked at her shockingly.

No, I can't come with you guys. I hate crowded places. I don't like noises. I don't like when people touch me. I am scared that I will get into my PYSCO behavior again.

" I.... Can't... I have a meeting " I managed to cover myself.

" Uncle please come with us. Let's enjoy together " Pumpkin said in sad tone. I looked at his cute little face. I looked at Avery helplessly.

" Ron, Go get changed. " Avery instructed.

" Is uncle not coming with us ? " Ron asked.

" He will " Avery said looking at me.

But....

I placed Ron on floor. He ran out of the kitchen.

" Avery.... I have a meeting.... Actually.... It's... " Before I speak. Avery started to prepare the breakfast.

" Don't you want me to cure you ? It's the first step " Avery said filling the glasses with milk.

" But.... "

" Fine. How about I take stefen with us ? " Avery said quickly looking at me.

That's all anger raised in me. My eyes are completely red.

I quickly pulled her hand tightly. I pushed her to the near by wall. I looked at her angrily.

" Stef.... " Before she speak. I pressed her throat tightly. Avery started to struggle. She can't able to breathe.

" I already told you to not mention any men name in front of me. You can planning to go out with him " I asked angrily pressing her throat hardly.

" M... Ike.... It's .... Me.... Avery.... I.... Can't.... Breathe "

What am I doing ? Killing my wife.

I am trying to kill Avery.

I quickly removed my hand. Avery started to cough.

" Why ? Why you are waking up the monster in me ? " I asked in angry tone. I hold her face small tears are in her eyes. I placed a small kiss on her forehead. Tear rolled in my eyes.

" You belong to me " I said angrily. Avery looked at me.

That's all. I turned my back and started to cry slowly.

Why I can't able to control myself ? I am letting my PYSCO in me coming out.

I pressed my lips tightly. The minute I closed my eyes tears rolled down.

Suddenly I felt a hand on my shoulder. I quickly wiped my tears.

" I will get ready " I diverted and about to go. Avery make me turned to her and hugged me.

Hug ? This hug is so warm.

Avery's hug is just so magical. I feel her body. I feel her heart beat.

This hug is so relaxing and just want to cry in her arms.

" It's okay to cry in front of me " She said. I pressed my lips to let out a cry. Tears rolled out my cheek.

" I just took Stefen name to make you react and feel free to let out the emotions. " She said hugging me and rubbing my back. In a second I broke the hug.

" I will be waiting in the car. Get ready " I said without looking at her and walked out from there.

Avery point of view.

" I am ready " Ron Said excitingly. He jumped on sofa and started to clap his hands. I smiled looking at him. He is so happy.

Ever since I came here I didn't seen him smiling like this.

" Let's go " suddenly I heard Mike voice. He wore casual wear Still he wore full sleeves.

I already seen his tattoos what's there to hide.

Whatever.

I nodded and I took Ron's hand. We walked out. There I seen his luxurious new model car. My eyes widen seeing the car.

" What happened ? " Suddenly Mike asked making me come to reality. I quickly shook my head. He opened the door for us.

We both got seated in his luxurious car. While ron seated on my lap. Mike took the drivers seat.

I already been in his car. But.... I now realised the beauty of this car. Because of all this PYSCO problem. Now it's time to cure him.

" What's your favourite food ? " Suddenly Mike asked breaking the silence in the car.

he wants to know about me ?

" Sis loves chocolates " Suddenly Ron shouted loudly.

Last night we both accepted to be friends. It's fine. I have to start conversation with him. It will be better to know him and easy to treat him.

" Chocolates ? " Mike laughed while driving.

Mike is laughing ? My god !!! It's a good sign.

He started teasing me now.

" What's bad in eating chocolates ? " I asked a little angrily. He stopped laughing.

" I... Mean you are not a kid Avery " He said controlling his laughing.

You....

" Food is not a chocolate pumpkin. What's your favourite food Avery ? " Mike asked in soft tone.

" Pumpkin ? When did you start calling him like this ? " I asked quickly.

Only I can call him whatever I want.

" I like when uncle calls me pumpkin " Ron said while smiling. We both looked at eachother. In a second we turned our faces.

Why are you staring at him idiot?

" You.... Still didn't answered my question " Mike asked.

" I... Love Dumplings " I said.

" Dumplings ? Good. What's your favourite colour ? " Mike asked while concentrating on road.

" Blue "

" Blue ? I thought mostly girls like pink " Mike asked while smiling.

He is completely different person.

I laughed.

I also has to ask him something.

" Then.... What your favourite food ? " I asked looking at him.

" I eat whatever I want. I don't have favourite in it. " He said while moving the stir wheel.

That's a little strange.

" Your colour ? "

" Black " he said quickly.

Ewww.... Black ? Looking at him ofcourse he likes black. His bedsheets. His room curtains. His walls every thing is black.

Right now he wore the black shirt.

" WE ARE HERE !!! " Suddenly Ron shouted loudly.

....

The minute we got inside the amusement park. I seen Mike can't able to look at people nor he can't able near those loud noises. When people started to touch him he started to get scared.

I seen Mike started to sweat. In a second I hold his hand tightly. Mike looked at me.

" I am here " I said and smiled. He hold my hand so tightly. His hand became cold.

" Uncle let's eat ice cream " Ron said and pulled Mike's hand. I gave nod to go. Mike looked at me helplessly.

" Avery.... I can't able to handle this crowed let's go home " Mike whispered slowly to me.

" You can do It Mike. I will make you do it " I said holding his hand tightly and in a second I let go off his hand. Ron dragged him to a shop. I stood there looking at both. The shop is so crowded that in a second I didn't seen Ron or mike. I ran towards the shop. I seen Mike came out of the crowed pressing his ears tightly.

" Mike, what happened ? " I panicked and ran to him and hold me. He started to breath badly. He is sweating and shaking. I hold his face with my hands.

" Mike look at me " I said. I seen him looking down and shivering.

" Mike ? Mike ? Are you listening ? "

" MIKE !!! " I yelled loudly. Mike looked at me.

" Take a deep breath " I said. Tears are in his eyes. He took a deep breath.

" Close your eyes "

" Now imagine that you are in empty street. There is no one. No noises. No people. Only you " I said.

" Now open your eyes " I said. The minute he opened his eyes. He looked at me. He looked around. He smiled.

" I feel relaxed. Now I feel normal Avery " He said and pulled me Into a tight hug.

I smiled and hugged him.

After a few minutes I realised.

Ron? Where is ron ?

" Mike ? where is Ron ? " I asked and broke the hug. Mike looked at me shockingly.

We looked around us. Ron I no where.

Panic started in me. That's all tears appeared in my eyes.

" Avery calm down. I will search him. I... Am sorry it's my fault " Mike said in sad tone.

I am not in a position to listen the explanation.

" RON.... RON.... " I started to shout. We both started to search him. After 5 minutes.

Where are you Ron ? You are the only one I have in my life.

" UNCLE !!! " Suddenly I heard a crying sound. As I turned around there I seen Ron. He is crying literally badly. While Mike hugged him tightly.

" I am sorry. It's uncle's fault. I won't leave you again " Mike said in sad tone.

" Superman " Ron just said that and hugged Mike tightly.

Superman ?

Mike smiled.

I ran to Ron and hugged him tightly.

" Where did you go ? you almost got me heart attack " I said angrily.

" It's my fault please don't scold him " Mike said sadly.

" No, it's not Superman's fault. Superman told me to hold his hand tightly but I seen Micky mouse and went to him. " Ron said.

" Fine. Lets go home " I said angrily.

" We still didn't spent time together " Mike said and lifted Ron in his arms.

" Yes " ron said wiping his tears.

Just now he made me heart attack.

" You.... " I started to make tickles to ron. While Mike is saving him.

After spending the two hours.

Mike is just so different today.

Will you be same when we go home or you gone be a monster again.

Suddenly I felt somebody hold my hand.

" Thank you " Mike said while having a smile on his face.

" It will be more beautiful when I see our wedding ring on your hand " Mike said showing me the hand which we both are holding. That's all tears appeared in my eyes.

" Hey ..." Mike hold my face while smiling. I placed my hands on my mouth.

" Why are you crying ? I can't see my best friend crying like this " He said while smiling at me.

" This moment here in this park .... You looked just like my dad " I said while crying. Mike pulled me into a tight hug.

" I... Wish I be like this forever " He said in sad tone.

Hey guys !!!

That's the end of the chapter.

Please do like, share, comment.

A beautiful night

Mike point of view

While me and pumpkin playing. Suddenly I seen Avery came into the room. I seen her face dull and weak.

What happened to her ?

" Ron, stop playing. It's already midnight let's sleep " Avery said a little angrily. Ron made a sad face.

" Uncle sleep with us " Ron said holding my hand tightly. I looked at Avery. She didn't responded and slept beside Ron.

What happened to her ? She was so happy on morning.

" Sis, Uncle will sleep here " Ron said waking up Avery.

" Ron... Let me sleep " Avery said. She turned to other side.

She don't like me to sleep here.

" Pumpkin , uncle have work to do. Why don't you sleep with sis ? " I said smiling at him.

" No, You will sleep with us. You promised me that you are going to tell me a bed time story " Ron said angrily and started to wake up Avery.

" Sis... Wake up... Sis... Sis... "

" STOP IT RON !!! " Suddenly Avery yelled loudly. I got shocked. Ron started to cry. While Avery walked out of the room.

I hugged Ron.

" Shh.... Sis must be tired. Don't cry. Tommorow you will get a bonus. Chocolates + story + lots of toys " I said. Ron stopped crying.

" Really ? "

I gave a nod.

" Come on !!! Now sleep. " I said and made him sleep.

What happened to Avery ?

After a few minutes I seen Ron slept. I covered him with blanket and switched on the bed light and walked out of the room.

I walked to my room. There I seen her on bed.

She is struggling to sleep. I went and got on the other side of bed.

I seen her sweating.

" Are you okay ? " I asked and bent slowly to look at her. I seen she frowned her eyebrows.

Did I do something again to her ?

" Avery, what happened ? Why did you yell at Ron ? " I asked slowly in worried.

" Please.... Leave me alone " She said. I slowly placed my hand on her shoulder.

" Avery talk to me. what happened ? You usually don't yell at Ron " I asked her. Suddenly I seen Avery woke up and ran into the washroom.

Is she sick ?

I ran behind her. I started to knock the door.

" Avery.... Avery.... Are you fine ? What's happening ? Why aren't you telling me anything ? " I started to call her.

Suddenly I seen the door opened. I seen her weak and dull. She is not opening her eyes properly. I quickly hold her.

" Are you sick ?" I asked and placed my hand on her forehead.

No, she dont have fever.

I made her sit on bed.

" Are you going to say or do you want me to call Stefen ? " I Asked angrily. She just placed her head down.

She won't say.

I pulled the phone. In a second Avery hold my hand. And nodded as no. I got kneel down. I took her hands. I looked into her eyes waiting for her answer.

" You.... Won't understand " She said.

Won't understand ? How can I not understand her ?

" We are friends. I can understand tell me. Did I do something again to you ? " I asked in sad tone.

" No... No... You didn't do anything. " She said quickly.

" Then... What ? " I asked in worried tone. She took a breath.

" My... My... Aunt came " She said hesitatly.

" Aunt ? You have aunt ? But you never said to me. What's big deal ? Let's invite her here " I said quickly. Avery looked at me angrily.

What ? I am solving her problem.

" What ? Is your relationship is not good with your aunt ? " I asked in worried tone. Avery about to get up.

" Where are you going ? We are not done yet " I warned her. Avery sat there helplessly.

" Mike.... Let me use washroom " Avery said and about to get up. I stopped her.

" You just used " I said. Avery hit her head with her hand.

" Calm down " I said and hold her hand. She ignored me and got up. And started to walk towards the washroom.

" AVERY !!! " I shouted. She turned to me.

" I AM ON PERIODS " She said angrily and walked into the washroom.

Period ? What it means ?

Avery point of view

I am already stressed and irritated. He is irritating me more.

Can't he get what aunt means ?

He knows how to kiss. He knows how to have sex. But.... Can't he even get aunt.

I walked out of the room. I looked around I didn't seen Mike anywhere.

Where did he go now ?

Finally I can get some sleep.

I am about to got to bed.

Suddenly I seen Mike came Into the room. He is holding ice pack, chocolates.

I looked at him shockingly.

" What all this ? " I asked while smiling.

" I just googled it. " Mike said placing them on table.

" What ? You just googled it. Seriously you don't know about it ? " I asked shockingly. Mike started to look around without me. I smiled.

" Sleep. I'm going to place it on your stomach " He said holding the ice pack.

He really don't know about it ?

How can it be ?

I lay on bed. Mike about to lift my shirt. I quickly stopped him.

" I... Can... Do it... " I said hesitatly.

" I... Am sorry " Mike said. He turned around. I quickly placed the ice pack and covered with my shirt.

I don't know suddenly I brust out laughing.

Mike looked at me.

" You.... Really don't know. " I said and started to laugh.

" Stop laughing " Mike said. I just started to laugh till my stomach started paining.

" Ah... " I whispered in pain. Mike quickly placed his hand on my stomach.

" Is it paining ? Chocolates. It's reduce the pain " Mike said quickly handing me the chocolates. I stopped laughing. I started to stare at him. We started to stare at each other.

Suddenly the ice pack slipped from my hand. It landed on floor. Mike quickly removed the hand. He both are so embrassing.

What have you done Avery ? Don't you get ? you are friends.

" I..... "

" I.... Will get some ice cubes " Mike said and quickly walked out of the room.

Idiot what have you done.

I walked out of the room. I got downstairs there I seen Mike seated on dining table.

" I... Am sorry... I didn't mean to... Make fun of you " I said.

" No, it's not your fault. It's just.... That I never dated anyone. Nor I never got close to any women. I know least about women. Actually I.... Don't have much friends. So.... I don't know all this. I.... Think... I am not a good husband for you. I always made you disappointed " He said. Suddenly I sensed his sad voice. I ran to him and hugged him from back.

He covered his mouth from stopping crying.

" I.... Am not qualified to be your husband. I only... Tortured you. When... I try to take care of you. I even don't know this simple thing " He said while crying. Tears rolled in my eyes.

" No.... No.... You are always the best. It's fine to not know. I... Am sorry " I said in tears. Mike turned to me.

" I... Am sorry " he said placing his hand on my face wiping my tears.

" Don't cry. I can't see you crying. " He said and attached my head with his head. We both started to cry.

I took a deep breath. I wiped my tears. I removed the hug.

I am crying in his arms. What happening to me ?

I am so embrassing.

Why I am blushing ?

I seen Mike wiped his tears.

" Do... You want to eat ice cream ? " Mike asked. I placed my head down and nodded. Mike walked into the kitchen.

Stupid Avery. You are blushing in front of him.

I know... I know.... He is changed now. He is completely fine now. But.... How can I have feelings for him ?

We promised to be friends.

Suddenly I heard my phone started ringing. I looked at the screen.

Dr. Stefen ? Why he is calling this late night ?

I quickly picked up the call.

" Yes, Dr. Stefen ? "

" Now we know Avery. Just call me stefen " He said on other side. I smiled.

" So, How is Mike ? Is he behaving strange again ? " He asked.

" No, he is completely fine. I took him to amusement park today. "

" What ? Park ? Did he really went to park ? I mean did he got used to the crowd ? " Stefen asked shockingly.

" Hmm... He is completely fine now. He told me that he is feeling great. I think he don't need medicines now " I said while smiling.

" Really ? How about you guys come to my hospital ? I want to check Mike to make sure he is completely fine. " He said.

" Sure. I will be there " I said.

" I said right your presence will cure him " Stefen said in soft tone. My smile faded.

Did I really cured him ? He suffered this many days and he finally got cured because of me.

" Are you there ? "

I blinked my eyes.

" Yes... Yes... See you tomorrow " I said and hung up the call.

I seen Mike holding a two cups of ice cream. I looked at him and smiled.

" Let's eat in the balcony " I said and got up.

" But.... It's cold outside " Mike said in worried tone.

" It's fine " I said and pulled the cups from his hand and moved to the balcony.

After a few minutes I seen Mike came holding a blanket in his hand.

I leaned on a small bed. The bed is so small. I just want to view the beautiful stars on the sky. Mike walked to me he covered me with blanket and about to sit on chair.

" Come here " I said patting beside me. Mike smiled and slept beside me.

The bed is so small we are so close together.

I am about to cover him with blanket.

" It's fine " Mike said. I ignored him and covered him with blanket. We started to eat ice cream.

" Dr. Stefen.... Just called " I said hesitatly.

To make sure he won't turn into monster again. He looked at me quickly.

" Did he say something ? " Mike asked quickly.

He didn't reacted. Mike is cured. Is he really cured ?

" Hey " Mike wave is hand in front of me. I came out of thoughts.

" He wants to take some tests " I said. Suddenly I seen Mike face turned into sad. I placed my hand on his palm.

" Are you okay ? " I asked looking at him. I seen small tears in his eyes.

" Ya... I am completely fine. " Mike said faking a smile.

" It will be fine. I am here " I said. Mike started to stare into my eyes. Suddenly we both started to stare at each other eyes. Suddenly I seen Mike came closer to my lips.

He wants to kiss me.

My heart started to beat. Why I am not refusing him ? I feel like to kiss him too.

Did I fell in love with this side of Mike ?

I felt his lips on my lips. He slowly started to move his lips.

He never kissed me like this. He always forced me. But now.... Right now.... It feels like good.

His lips are slowly moving on my lips. He just kissing me slowly. His hands ran towards my waist to pull me closer.

I closed my eyes feeling his lips. In a second I too started to move my lips.

Suddenly Mike stopped kissing. His lips got away from me. The minute I opened my eyes. Mike started to look into my eyes he frowned his eyebrows.

Why did you stopped ? Is he not okay with it ?

He just got up

" It's... Late... Let's sleep " Mike said breaking his words. We are both embrassed.

He kissed me many times. But... This kiss is completely different.

Mike is about to get up.

" Let's sleep here " I said in one go. Mike stopped turned to me.

" Huh ? " He is confused. I just placed my head down. While Mike got seated and leaned on bed. I too slept beside him.

" I wish I will I never turn into monster again " Mike said. I can feel his voice is sad. I looked at him..while Mike staring at stars.

He is feeling guilty. I have to say to him that I fell in love with him.

" Mike, I.... " Before I speak. Mike pulled me closer to his chest.

" Sleep. It's late " He said and pulled me more closer to him.

I really fell in love with you Mike. Whatever the reason may be. From today i am going to handle you.

I hope I killed the monster in you.

That's the end of the chapter. Please do like, share, comment.

Please don't be a readers. Just drop your comments. I too get the hope to write more episodes.

Party

Mike point of view

We are right now in Stefen's hospital. Avery sat beside me. While stefen sat infront of us.

" So, what's the reports say ? " Avery asked quickly. Stefen stood from the chair.

" One last test " Stefen said and came towards me. He placed his hand on my shoulder. He pulled out a medicines bottle from his pocket. He placed it in front of me.

That's all panic attacked me. I started to sweat. I am trying my best to not let anything go wrong today.

I... Am going to fight this. I am going to let me free. I am going to kill the monster in me.

I have to....

I looked at Avery. Her eyes looked at me worried. She took my hand slowly.

Get through this for you Avery. I will. I will.... For Ron, For you. For our future.

I get out the breath. I felt relaxed. I closed my eyes and opened it. I looked at the medicines on his hand.

" How do you feel Mike ? Are you still getting tensed, panicked, anger ? Come on !!! Say it " Stefen asked. Avery and stefen are Eagerly waiting for my answer.

I smiled.

" I feel normal " Stefen and Avery smiled. Avery hugged me tightly.

Avery hugged me. She... Is not scared of me. I got through all this.

" You are fine. You are completely fine " Avery said holding my face in her hands. I seen small tears are in her eyes. I smiled and nodded.

Happy tears are both in our eyes.

" Party is must " Stefen said while smiling. Suddenly Avery and me realized that we are close together. We removed back.

She thinks we are best friends. I can't let my feelings come out.

After what I have done. I can't expect love from her.

" Of course. Party is on. Today 9:00 pm at my home. Be ready " I said.

" That's my bro. You are back man. " Stefen said and punched on my chest. We started to laugh.

Avery point of view

He is back. Mike Wilson is back.

Why I am continuously staring at him ?

What's happening to you Avery ?

He kissed you many times. Why are still got stuck on last night kiss ?

You guys already slept on same bed. Then why last night means so much to you ?

Why i am changing my feelings towards him ?

" Avery ? " I came out of my thoughts when I heard Mike calling me.

" Are you okay ? Stefen asked you something " Mike asked in worried tone.

" Sorry... Actually... I am thinking about something else. what did you say stefen ? " I smirked. Stefen and mike looked at me confused.

" I.....asked do you drink ?" stefen asked smiling at me.

" i prefer only red wine " I said. Both laughed.

"sure. whatever you like " stefen said.

" Stefen, Didn't i told you to...... " suddenly a lady got into the room. She stopped talking when she seen mike. She is beautiful. She will be around my age. Her tummy is out. Looks like she is pregnant around 5 months.

" Why he is here ?" she asked angrily looking at stefen. I looked at mike who is about to get close to her.

" Tell him that i don't want to talk to him " She said angrily. She didn't looked at mike while mike is just staring at her sadly. Mike walked to her and placed his hand on her shoulder.

" He is cured, Ana " stefen said. In a second she looked at mike and hugged him tightly in tears. Mike hugged her too.

" I know you will be cured " She said in tears.

who is she? Is she mike's girlfriend ? The baby in her stomach. Is it mike's.

tears started in my eyes. They started to smile at each other. Everything went blank. I can't able to hear anything. I seen them laughing at each other. Mike kissed her cheek. He bent down and started to talk with baby in her belly.

Why stefen didn't told me that mike has a girlfriend ? She is pregnant.

A pain hit in my heart.

" I.... missed you " Mike said and hugged her again.

Before i realise my eyes filled with tears.

I just started to have feelings for him. Why did it happened now ? why ? why ?

" avery... avery.... avery " suddenly i heard someone patting my shoulder.I came out of thoughts. I seen mike, stefen and the lady started to stare at me in confused. I seen a tear dropped down my cheek.

" What happened ? Why are you crying ?" mike asked in concerned. I looked at him and quickly wiped my tears.

" something got into my eyes " i said and smiled. Mike took my face in his hands and slowly wiped my tears with his thumb.

" Is your stomach paining ?" he whispered slowly to me. I nodded as no and smiled.

No, My heart is paining.

" Is something disturbing you ?" Mike asked.

" Who is she ?" Suddenly the lady asked quickly. Mike placed his hand around my shoulder. She looked at us.

" she is...." Before mike speak more. I quickly removed his hand.

" His friend, Avery " I said. I seen stefen and mike looked at me in confused. Mike looked at me shockingly.

No, i can't let her know this marriage. She is carrying mike's child.

" Friend ? " She asked suspiciously. I smiled and gave her my hand to shake.

" Avery, What are you saying ?" stefen asked shockingly.

what i have to say ? i am helping you guys.

she came closer to me. she didn't made the handshake. She looked at me angrily. My heart started to beat fastly. In a second she pulled mike collar tightly. My eyes widen in shock.

" YOU HAVE A GIRLFRIEND " She shouted loudly in anger. I quickly made them stop.

" Please..... don't do anything to him. " I said in tears.

" She is my wife, Ana" Mike said and smiled.

he is smiling ? is he crazy ? Is he not going to take the responsibility.

" WIFE ?" she shouted again.

No.....I have to stop.

I quickly kneel in front of her.

" I will divorce him. I will leave him. He will take responsibility. Don't hurt him. He will take care of his baby " I said in tears.

" WHAT ? " She shouted shockingly.

" responsibility ?" stefen shocked.

" Avery, What are you saying ?" Mike said shockingly and quickly made me get up.

" Excuse me. She is my wife. I can take care of my child " stefen said quickly and place his arm around her shoulder.

Huh ? she is stefen's wife.

You are idiot avery. now answer them.

" She is my sister. It's not my child. It's stefen's " Mike said and started laughing.

Sister ?

Mean while i seen stefen and her wife too started laughing loudly.

" what.... what got you think that i am his girlfriend and baby is his ?" She said while laughing

I just placed my head down in embarrassed.

mike looked at me while smiling.

" You.... both hugged each other " i said.

" Can't siblings hug each other ?" she said while smiling. Mike looked at me and smiled.

" Avery, She is Ana my wife. Ana, she is Avery Mike's wife. " Stefen came forward and introduced us. I smirked.

I messed everything up.

" Hello " Ana came forward and we both shake the hands.

" I.... Am sorry. I misunderstood. He never told me that he as little sister " I said and smiled. She looked at Mike.

" We are not biological. We met when Mike use to come here for treatment. He always been my best brother. " She said smiling at mike.

" He use to keep me far away. He was scared that he might hurt me " She said a little sadly.

" You got married and didn't informed me " Ana said angrily and gave a punch on his chest.

" Ouch !!!! If I told you I am going to marry, You won't let me. You know my condition On that time " Mike said Rubbing his chest slowly.

" You...... " She is about to hit again. Stefen stopped.

" Ana, That's enough " Ana looked at stefen angrily.

" I am going to hit you. You didn't informed me too " She said angrily and hit his husband head.

" Ah.... I am about to say you " Stefen said pouting his lips. She got stefen's ear tightly.

" Ah... Ah... Ana, I am your husband " He said in pain.

" When are you going to tell me ? When they have children ? "

My eyes widen in shock. Me and Mike felt inconvenient.

" Ana, Stop !!!! We are throwing a party tonight. You guys have to come " Mike spoke up. Ana stopped.

" Fine " She said.

" We will see at home " She said angrily to stefen Mike laughed. I smiled.

They look adorable. I didn't expect that stefen is married that too he is going to be a father.

" We are leaving. Ron will be back from school " Mike said. I pulled my purse.

" You..... Guys have baby too " Ana said shockingly. She is about to hit Mike.

" Cool, Ana. She is Avery's brother. He is 5 years old "

Ana relaxed.

We said goodbyes.

....

Right now we are in car.

Should I ask about my questions to him.

He said he never had friends. But.... He as such a great friends just like a family.

He never told me about Ana too.

" Do you want to ask something ? " He asked while driving.

" Ana... She.... " I hesitated to ask him.

" When I met stefen they use to date each other. Ana always been my little sister. But.... After a year. I use to avoid her because.... I don't want to hurt her. I... Got scared to lose another family member " He said sadly.

Should I tell him that I read his dairy. Will he get angry.

" I seen her today after 2 years " He said.

" 2 years ? That's so long " I said shockingly.

" That's why she got so angry. If not she is just so funny. She always make people around her happy. Stefen is lucky to have her " Mike continues.

I am no use. I am not a perfect wife.

Do I say him about dairy ?

" Mike " I called him.

" Hmm " He concentrated on driving.

It's not right time to tell. He is so happy.

" Nothing " I said.

" Feel free to ask questions about me. Let's get to know each other more " Mike said and gave a look at me.

We didn't talked about the kiss last night.

I know he loves me. He always loved me. It will be awkward if I said him that I am falling in love with him.

I stared at Mike . Mike looked at me. I quickly turned my face.

Why I keep staring at him ?

It's got complete silence for 5 minutes.

" I...was so happy. when you supported me in hospital. It's good to know that I some what have a place in your heart " Mike said breaking the silence. I smiled.

" what you guys love to eat ? I will make it tonight for party. " I said excitingly. Mike smirked.

" We have lots of servants. It's time for you to rest. You have struggled so much for Ron's future. Now let me handle it. " Mike said while smiling.

That's it. My heart felt something weird. Butterflies started in my stomach.

He even know that I struggled all this time.

" I researched on you. When I married you " He added. My eyes widen in shock.

He is telling all his secrets. Don't I think I should tell him too about his dairy.

" Mike.... " Before I continue.

" We are here " Mike said and stopped the car. I looked outside. We are back to home.

When I am going to say to him ?

....

The clock stricked 9:00pm. The party started. I looked myself in mirror. I wore the red long fork.

It's looks like expensive. I am not used to this dresses.

But, The dress is comfortable. It's just shining brightly in light.

Last and finally I put my ear rings. I smiled.

When I am going to say him about his dairy ?

I walked downstairs only to find Mike stood there. He wore the black suit.

Black again ?

He looks just handsome and stunning.

He just started to stare at me.

" You look beautiful " Ana said coming towards me. I smiled.

Is he not going to say anything ?

" Let's start the party " Stefen shouted and he quickly pulled the bottle cork and pour in glasses.

" Where is Ron ? I am so excited to see him " Ana asked looking around.

" There he is " Mike said pointing his finger. There Ron playing him toys.

" Pumpkin, come here " mike called Ron. He ran to Mike. Mike quickly lifted him.

" Pumpkin, She is aunt Ana, say hi " Mike said.

" Hi aunty " Ron said with his cute little voice.

" He is so cutee... " Ana said and pinched softly Ron's cheek. Ron blushed. Mean while stefen came to.

" Here Uncle Stefen. " Mike pointed.

" I seen him. It's first time talking to him. Hello super hero " Stefen said.

" Hello uncle "

" Now go play " Mike said and put him on ground. Ron ran towards the toys.

" I am going to get starters. " I said and walked into the kitchen.

" Let me come too " Ana followed me. We both started to arrange the plates.

" stefen said that you cured Mike. Thank you " Ana said a little emotionally.

" He made it. I just helped him. It's not my credit " I smiled. Ana smiled.

" I don't know what he done to you. But.... What ever he done. It's not him Avery. Please forgive him. I never seen him smiling like this. " Ana said. I nodded.

I already forgiven him.

We walked towards the dinning table. I placed all the dishes on table and sat beside Mike. While Ana told seated beside stefen.

Stefen started to fill wine in all our glasses. He took Ana's glass.

" Alcohol is prohibited to you. Drink juice " Stefen warned.

" I know "

" Let's cheers for the Mike cure " Stefen yelled. We all clicked our glasses. I am about to take a sip.

" You can handle wine right ? " Mike whispered slowly.

Of course I can. I am not a kid.

" Of course. I am expert in it " I said and about to complete the glass at once.

" Slowly. Eat this " Mike said and placed the chicken fry into my plate. I took it.

....

After a few hours.

" May I have a dance with you ? My lady " stefen said. Ana took his hand. The room is filled with music.

They started to dance. He made sure he took a small steps to take care of ana. While I seen Mike stared at me. He signalled me to dance. I blushed.

Background romantic song is played.

Mike came to me. He took my hand. Mike slowly pulled my waist. He inter linked our finger. We slowly started to take steps.

I just placed my head down.

" Avery " Mike called.

" Hmm " I lifted my head. I looked into his eyes.

" Do you forgive me ? " He asked in sad tone.

" For what ? " I asked.

" For everything I have done for you " He said. I smiled.

" I Have forgiven you already " I said. Mike looked at me shockingly. I seen tears rolled in his eyes. Suddenly Mike hugged me.

" Are you okay ? " I asked. He just tested his head on my shoulder.

....

" Avery it's enough " She is drunk. I pulled the glass from her hand. She pouted.

" He... Is not letting me drink " She started to cry like baby.

" I made Ron sleep. He is sleeping " Ana said. I nodded.

" Are you sure you can handle her ? " Stefen asked.

" I can " I nodded. Then both ana and stefen left the house. While I looked at Avery she is drunk and playing with bottles. I went to her.

" Get up. Let's go upstairs " i said and about to pull her up.

" No, I want one more bottle " She said and sat on ground.

" If I know you behave like this. I wouldn't have let you drink alcohol " I said.

" Come. Sit here..... We.... We have lots to talk tonight " Avery said patting beside her. I sat. I looked at her beautiful face.

She is cute when she is drunk. I smiled. She is about to drink again. I stopped her. In a second I looked at her finger.

" You still didn't wear the wedding ring ? " I asked sadly.

She looked at her finger.

" Ring ? Where.... Did it go ? .... I remember now I throwed it. " She said. A pain hit in my heart. My eyes widen in shock. Tears rolled in my eyes.

You just throwed our wedding ring.

Do You hate me so much Avery ?

Do you still want us to be friends ?

Dont you feel anything for me Avery ?

That's the end. Hope you guys like it. Please comment me. I hope you love the chapter.

I seen mostly people just voting me. Please don't just read it. Express your views on it.

As a writer i feel disappointed

Please comment me. I love to view your comments.

I make sure I read evey ones comment and improve myself and let you reach your standards.

Love you all !!!!

She is drunk

Mike point of view

" Lets go upstairs " I said and about to get up. Avery pulled my hand I feel on her. She looked at me with her beautiful eyes. Her cheeks red and her lips are pink.

I tried to kiss her. I stopped.

No... No.... I won't repeat my mistakes.

I sat beside her.

" You are beautiful tonight " I said looking into her eyes.

" I... Waited for you to say " She said. I chuckled.

" Do you know ? I used to be scared of you. " She said. She is completely drunk.

I know.

" But...... Now.... I am not scared of you. You became so gentle. But.... " She stopped. I am eagerly waiting for to continue. She made a sad face.

" I am scared of your dangerous room" she said in sad tone.

The room which I took Avery to. I will renovate that room so beautifully that Avery will be shocked to see that.

I will make you happy as much as I can. I will be the new Mike Wilson.

I can't let you see my monster again. Never and ever.

" Avery, Do you hate me ? " I want to confirm it.

She looked at me.

" Why would I ? I used to be. But, Not now " she said and smiled at me. She is about to pull the wine bottle again. I stopped.

" Avery, you are drunk " I stopped. She looked at me with those pity eyes. Suddenly she took my face in her hands.

" I... I.... " Before she speak. She vomited badly on my shirt.

Avery....

I am about to lift her in my arms. She refused.

" No, I am going to sleep here tonight " She pouted. I smiled.

I walked to my room and quickly changed my shirt. I pulled a pair of clothes for Avery and got down.

The minute I got down. I shocked to see Avery in our mini bar. She is drinking again. I ran to her.

" Avery " I called and pulled the bottle from her hand.

" Mike.... One sip " She said in sad tone. I pulled her shoulders.

" Shh.... Change your clothes. " I said and handed her clothes. She made a sad face. I placed my hand on her head and smiled.

Suddenly she started to remove her shirt. I quickly turned back.

" Avery, change in room " I said.

" No.... I will change here. Don't you dare turn back " She warned. I smiled.

" Fine. Change it. I won't look " I said.

After a few minutes.

" Done " Avery yelled. The minute I turned. I shocked to see Avery Placed the buttons randomly.

I laughed.

" Is it the way to put buttons ? " I laughed. She looked at the buttons helplessly. I walked to her and started to put the buttons neatly.

Suddenly Avery leaned closer to me.

" I.... Have a secret of you " She whispered slowly in my ear. I smiled.

" Really ? What is it ? " I asked placing her buttons.

" I.... Read your dairy " She said. My eyes widen in shock. I stopped buttoning her. I raised my head. I seen Avery placed her head down.

She knows everything about me. She still not got scared of me. He helped me.

" I.... Am sorry... " She said sadly and placed her head down. Small tears appeared in my eyes. I quickly pulled her into a tight hug.

I controlled my tears and broke the hug. I wiped my tears.

" Who gave you my dairy ? " I asked.

" Stefen " She said sadly. I smiled.

" It's fine. You are my wife. You have every right to know about me " I said.

" Now, Sit here. I am going to get some milk. " I said. And made her sit on sofa. I walked to kitchen.

I can see her from kitchen. She is just like a small child now.

Even in drunk. She is just beautiful.

Suddenly my phone begin to buzz.

It's stefen.

" Is she ok ? Ana is just so worried " Stefen asked. I smiled.

" She is fine. She is about to sleep " I said and pour the milk in a glass.

" Thank god !!!! I thought she is going to kill you tonight " I chuckle.

" Are you going to work tomorrow ? " Stefen asked.

" Yes, I just want to make everything right. I want to communicate with people. I want to develop my company. I want to live a happy life with Avery and Ron " I said.

" Hey, you really changed idiot. Are you going to propose to Avery now ? "

My smile faded.

" I don't think so " I said sadly.

" What ? Are you guys going to stay just like that ? Being friends forever. She have feelings for you Mike. I can see it. In hospital she got jealous. Believe me. She is falling in love with you " stefen said.

" I can't take any step that will make her sad again. If she wants us to be friends. I will be her best friend forever " I said.

" You are idiot Mike. You going to let your feelings be with you and take care of her forever. Just let her know. She is fine with you now. " Stefen said.

" I... Already made her in a situation where I regret so much. She... Is now so happy with us, being friends. I don't want to ruin it. I.. am scared she will leave me. I don't want to leave alone again, not without her " I said. Small tears are in My eyes.

" But... " Before stefen speak further.

" What my little sister is doing ? " I diverted.

" She is sleeping " Stefen said. Suddenly I heard a loud sound from hall.

" What's that sound ? " Stefen asked.

" I will call you later " I said and hung up the call. I looked that Avery is not on sofa.

Where did she go ?

I ran out. I seen the vase is broken. I looked around. My heart started to beat. Panic started.

" Avery " i called. Suddenly I heard a voice behind the sofa. There I seen her hiding. I exhaled my breath.

This girl will make me worry.

" What are you doing there ? " I asked a little angrily.

I don't want to be angry at her. But, I have to warn her.

" I.... Didn't... Mean to break the vase. It... Slipped from my hand " She said and started to cry. I walked to her. I lifted her in my arms just like a small baby. She started to cry on my shoulder.

I placed her on sofa.

" Didn't I told you to sit on sofa and don't move " I said looking into her eyes and wiping her tears.

" Stop crying. " She hugged me. I slowly started to rub her hair.

" Now, Drink milk and go to sleep " I said and broke the hug. She nodded wiping her tears. She drank the milk.

" Finished " Avery said. I smiled. Suddenly in second she pulled my face and kissed my lips.

My eyes widen in shock. I removed her and turned my face.

She is drunk.

" Sleep " I said and about to get up. Avery hold my hand.

" No, I want to kiss you " She said. My eyes widen in shock.

She don't know what she is saying.

" Avery, sleep " I said. Avery got up. She is about to kiss me again.

" STOP IT !!! " I shouted. Avery got shocked and started crying.

She is drunk. I should make her understand and not yell at her.

I took her face in my hands.

" Don't cry. I.. am sorry. You are drunk Avery. You won't remember tomorrow all this. I don't want to do anything to regret again " I said sadly. She just crying. I can't able to see her cry.

I pulled her lips.

Yes, I kissed her.

I started to move my lips slowly. I pulled Avery waist. I seen Avery started to respond to me.

Why she wants to kiss me ? Why ?

I closed my eyes. I just kissing her more. Her soft lips making me want more.

The kiss sounds are filled in our room. Suddenly I seen Avery is going out of control. I stopped kissing. She is moving forward to my lips. I stopped her. My breath is touching her lips which is wet now.

" Not now " I said. Avery came closer to my lips again. I stopped.

" Avery listen. We will do it. Once you will be ready " I said sadly.

" I... Am ready " She said and about to kiss me.

" You are drunk. I don't want to regret it. I promise you that I will make our night so beautiful, when you be ready" I said and attached our foreheads.

I kissed her forehead and made her sleep on sofa.

Avery point of view

I opened my eyes slowly.

Ah.... My head. It's paining.

What happened ? I got drunk last night.

Did anything happened ? I quickly looked at my clothes.

His shirt. Why I am wearing his clothes ?

Something happened last night. What happened ? I started to think.

I looked around. I am in hall. Sofa ? Why I am sleeping on sofa ?

I found a piece of note on table. I picked it.

" Dont think anything. Nothing happened last night.

I prepared breakfast have it. I dropped Ron at school. I went to office will be back tonight at 8:00pm

Yours friendly

Mike Wilson "

What ? Friendly ? He thinks we are friends. I am trying to propose him. He is treating as a friend.

....

I prepared dinner for Mike. I sat on dinning table watching the clock.

It's 8:30pm.

Why Mike still not came ?

Suddenly the door bell rang. I ran towards door. I inhaled my breath. I smiled and opened the door.

" You didn't slept yet ?" Mike asked. I nodded as no. He walked in.

" Is Ron sleeping ? " Mike asked.

" No, He is playing upstairs " I said.

" I... Prepared breakfast. Let's get together " My stared at me for a second and nodded.

" I will change "

He walked upstairs.

Today I am going to say him about dairy.

I have to. He trust me now. I can't let him down.

....

After a few minutes I seen Ron walked downstairs. Ron is with him. Ron ran to me. I smiled and kissed his cheek.

We all got seated.

" Ron, Seat straight " I warned. Ron sat straight. Ron about to hold the hot soap on his plate. I stopped him.

" It's hot " I said and took it and blow it slowly and started to feed Ron.

" Is it good ? " I asked.

" I like it " Ron said.

" Do you always feed him ? " Suddenly Mike asked. I turned to him.

" No, He usually eat my himself. The food is hot so.. " Mike smiled and nodded. She took a spoon full of rice with chicken.

I am waiting for him to answer.

" How is it ? " I asked.

" Delicious, As always " he said. I blushed.

You are blushing idiot.

After we had dinner together.

" Sis, Bed time story " Ron said and started to pull my shirt. I smiled.

" Fine. Fine "

I looked at Mike who is busy in work. I don't want to disturb him. I will talk to him when he is free . Me and Ron walked upstairs.

Mike point of view

I closed my laptop. I stretched my arms. I looked around. I didn't seen Avery or Ron.

I walked upstairs. I didn't seen Avery in our room.

She still wants to sleep in Ron's room.

I walked to Ron's room. The door is opened slightly. I peeped.

" Finally the monster is killed " Avery said and closed the book.

" Now, come on sleep " She said.

" Sis, I want puppy " Suddenly pumpkin said.

" Puppy ? Why ? "

" My friend as huge dog. I want dog too " Ron said. Avery smiled.

" Ron, I know you love dogs. But.." ron made a sad face.

" Fine. I will talk to uncle. If he agrees Let's get one ok " Ron jumped on bed.

I smiled looking at the bond of sis and a brother.

She take care of Ron just like a mother.

I always dreamed of family. Finally I got it.

But.... How beautiful will it be when we have baby together. I started to think.

I mind clicks a photo.

I came out of thoughts. I seen Avery about to come out of the room. I stood outside. Avery looked at me.

" Is your work done ? " Avery asked. I nodded.

" You didn't slept yet ? "

" Ron, keep on asking me to tell him a story "

" Then... I will go to my room " I said.

" Let me come to " Avery said. My eyes widen in shock.

" Huh ? " I got confused.

" What ? Should I not sleep in your room ? " Avery asked.

" No... It's not that... " I said.

After kissing her twice. I feel awkward.

I know she won't remember last night.

We walked to our room.

" You can sleep on bed. I am going to sleep on floor " I said and about to pull my blanket.

" Do you think I am scary ? " Avery asked while smiling. I am about to speak.

" Sleep on bed. I will sleep on right. you sleep on other side " Avery said. My eyes widen in shock.

She told us to sleep on same bed.

I nodded. We both slept on our sides.

I wish I filled this gap between is Avery. I wish we have a family.

I can't able to bare this gap between us. As long as you accept me. I will wait for you.

I will wait for you Avery.

Thats the end. I hope you guys like it.

Please do like, share and comment. Your comments means a lot to me.

confess.

A very point of view

Today I am going to say him the truth. I am going to propose Mike.

We are not friends Mike. I love you. I fell in love with you.

Mike Is in office.

I prepared the candles, roses, cake everything is prepared.

" Ana, Do you think Mike will like it ? " I asked. While Ana is helping me to decorate.

" Don't worry. He loves you. You already know it. He is just waiting for your answer " Ana said Placing the roses petals on bed.

It's embrassing. It's just awkward to confess to Mike.

" Ana, There is no need to decorate bed " I said. Ana looked at me.

" Stupid girl !!! He loves it. Take this step further " Ana said.

I am just so nervous. My lips started shivering. I started to play with my hands.

Ana came to me and took my hand.

" Don't feel embrassed. Its fine to love someone. That too Mike is your husband idiot" Ana said. I smiled.

" Every thing is prepared downstairs " Stefen ran into the room.

" Cake " Ana asked.

" Done " Stefen replied.

" Flowers "

" Done "

" Candles "

" Done "

" Food " Stefen stopped.

" I know you will forget. Now go place them on dinning table. " Ana warned. Stefen ran down. I laughed.

" Thank you for helping me. Stefen didn't told Mike right ? " I asked.

" We are friends Avery. Cool. He didn't told anything to Mike " Ana said.

We started to decorate again. Suddenly ana pulled something from her purse. I didn't seen it clearly. She quickly placed it under the pillow.

" What's that ? " I asked. And about to look. Ana stopped me.

" It's..... scent. " Ana said quickly.

Why she look suspicious ?

" By the way. I am going to take Ron with us. We are going to drop him here at morning " Ana said.

" It's... Fine " before I complete. Ana came to me and hit my head.

" Ouch !!! Stupid girl. Can't you get it ? " Ana said. I started to rub my head.

No way....

I am just confessing to him. Not that.

I am still not yet prepared.

" But... "

" Shh.... We are taking him that's all. " Ana ordered. I nodded helplessly. We both walked downstairs. Stefen decorated beautifully.

" Let's go. It's time for mike to come. Come on boy " Stefen said and lifted Ron.

" Don't trouble uncle and aunt ok ? " I warned Ron. He nodded quickly.

" All the best. " Ana whispered. I blushed.

" Make baby too. Ron want's brother or sister right ? Ron " Stefen said while smiling. My eyes widen in shock. Ron nodded quickly while smiling.

Ana went to him and hit his back.

" Ana " stefen called in pain.

" Its there personal. Let's go. " Ana said a little angrily. Stefen pouted. They left the house.

The minute they left the house. I started to explore the house.

I wish I don't mess anything up.

I looked at my night pants.

I have to change. I got into my room.

I found a black dress on the bed.

Who kept it here ?

There is a note on it.

" I am serious. You are going to wear this dress. It's not.... Forget that we are friends   Ana. "

I smiled and picked up the dress.

My mouth widen looking at the dress.

It's so short and the neck is so deep. I never wore this kind of clothes.

Suddenly my phone buzzed. It's ana. I picked up.

" Ana this... " Before I speak.

" I know you are going to avoid it. But... I am serious. You have to wear it. If not, I have to going to reveal your surprise to Mike " Ana said seriously.

" It's black mail " I said helplessly.

" Its worth it. Come on. Wear it and send me that photo " Ana ordered.

She hung up the call.

Fine. There is no other choice. I picked up the dress. I changed into it.

The neck is so deep that my cleavage is clearly visible and it as no sleeves.

The dress is above my knees.

Ana.... I am going to kill you. I took a picture and sent it.

No... I have to change. Before I do that. Suddenly I heard someone opened the door. I turned around.

Is Mike back ? Idiot. Stefen and ana you guys didn't locked the main door.

My eyes widen. I am about to change quickly. Suddenly the zip is so tight that I can't able to remove it.

Damn zip. Why this dress is so tight ?

" Avery " I heard Mike's voice from downstairs. I helplessly walked downstairs.

Mike point of view

I am about to knock the door. I seen that it's opened.

Avery would never left the door opened.

I walked inside. I shocked to see the whole house is dark. Suddenly I stepped on something.

I seen filled with beautiful dim lights, candles, roses. The candle light dinner. The special foods placed on table.

Who prepared all this ? Avery ?

Why would Avery do that ?

" Avery " i called. After a few minutes. I seen Avery coming downstairs.

My eyes widen. She wore black dress. She just looks so sexy and beautiful.

Sexy ? Stupid Mike.

She never wore this kind of dress.

She walked to me slowly. She is trying her best to cover her cleavage and knees.

I... Had seen her body. But.... I don't remember all those days. It's feels like a first time to see Avery like this.

She is now in front of me.

" I... Just... " She hesitated. I am just staring at her beautiful face. Her eyes. Her lips.

She lowered her eyes.

" Did you prepared all this ? " I asked looking at avery.

" No, Ana and stefen helped me. " She just not even looking at my face. I felt that she is just not comfortable with her dress.

" Why don't you change it ? " I said and smiled. She looked at me shockingly.

" Don't.... Don't... You like it ?" She asked in sad tone. I slowly removed her hair locks behind her ear.

" You are beautiful. You are so beautiful that I won't control myself when I see you in this dress " I said looking at her. She got shocked.

" I... Will.... Change " With that she ran upstairs. I chuckled.

....

I got fresh up. Avery got downstairs she got changed into a night pants. I smiled.

She walked to me.

" Is something special ? " I asked looking into her eyes.

Say it Avery. I am waiting for the damn answer.

" I... I.... " She hesitated. I suddenly seen her lips started to shiver. She is so nervous placing with her fingers. I went close to her and made her look into my eyes. Her eyes started blinking.

" Whatever is it, say it. Don't be scared...... " Before I continue.

" I READ YOUR DAIRY !!! " She shouted. Smile on my face faded.

You did all this just to say this. I thought you are going to confess to me.

" I.... Know it's wrong. But... " She started to say. I moved back from her. A pain hit in my heart.

" You.... Did all just to say this ? " I asked in sad tone. Small tears rolled in my eyes.

" It's... " Before she complete.

" I know. You already said when you are drunk. You don't need to apologize. Just.... " I said in tears. I turned back and can't able to control my tears.

You just want to say this.

Suddenly I felt a pair of hands around my waist. I am about to turn.

" Don't turn " Avery said.

" I... Can't say it when I look into your eyes " She said. I can hear that she is crying.

" I love you Mike. " She uttered. My eyes widen. I am just so happy tears started to drop down my cheek.

" It's not just about dairy. I prepared all this just to say this " She said. I removed the back and turned to her. She placed her head down. I seen her eyes full of tears. I took her face in my hands.

" Say it again " I said. Avery looked at me.

" I love you mike. I fell in love with you " She said while smiling. I pulled her into a tight hug. We both hugged for a long time.

I broke the hug and looked at her face. I wiped her small tears. I smiled.

" Let's eat. You prepared so many " I said. She nodded.

After we had dinner.

" What do you want to do next ? " I asked. We both seated on sofa exploring the dim light.

We just sat so far.

Suddenly Mike pulled my waist. I looked at him shockingly.

" Its good now " Mike smiled. I blushed. I just started to stare at her. Suddenly I kissed her. Slowly we started to kiss.

I pulled her more closer to me.

Avery loves me. She loves me.

I am just feeling her lips. My kiss Started to be more passionate. We are going out of control.

I don't know when we landed on our bed. I am on top of avery. I looked at her beautiful face.

I looked at bed it's decorated with roses

" Didn't told me you want this ? " I asked in shock.

Avery point of view

it's not mine idea.

Ana..........

I lowered my eyes. I am blushing.

really ?

" Ana.... Done it. " I barley spoke.

He is on top of me.

its embarrassing....

" Will........... you get off me ? " I said hesitantly. Mike got confused.

"It's... awkward " I said lowering my eyes. Mike chuckled. He got me and started to laugh.

what happened ?

"we.... are in a such a romantic mood and you.... " Mike started laughing. I blushed.

can't people get embarrassed. He was top of me.

" Stop... " I said placing my hand on his mouth. mike is laughing loudly. I started to hit him. We started to fight on bed.

" Stop laughing " I said. Mike pulled the pillow for protecting. Suddenly something dropped from bed. Mike bent to look into. Suddenly he looked at me shockingly.

what's there ?

" what ?" i asked looking at him. Mike pulled up.

My eyes widen in shock.

whats that doing here ?

ANA..... I AM GOING TO KILL YOU.

" I didn't thought you are this fast " Mike said while smiling and showing me.

Condom packet

what kind of stupid plan is this ana ?

" look....It's not me. Ana.... " before i complete. Mike pulled my waist.

"mike... It's not me "I said struggling myself to get out of his grip.

"so,what ? Let's continue before it's gets waste " Mike said coming closer to my lips. I stopped.

" Mike.... " I warned. We started to laugh.

We started to keep on laughing. Suddenly i seen mike stopped laughing and started to stare at me.

" w_hat... " Mike in a second he came close to my lips.

He grabbed my lips. We started to kiss slowly.

We are just kissing not more than that. Suddenly mike made me lay on bed.

Is it going to happen now ?

He started kissing me slowly. Suddenly his hands ran into my shirt. I gasped. Mike looked at me.

He raised his eyebrows for my answer. I just blushed. mike smiled. He got down and slowly lifted my shirt. I am just so into him. suddenly a moan escaped from my mouth.

Mike about to place kiss on my stomach. Suddenly i seen he stopped. I looked at him.

I shocked to see tears in his eyes.

That's the end. Hope you guys like it. Next chapter is going to be so bold(18+). Read at your own risk.

love

This chapter is 18+

I suggest it's not suitable for below 18

It's totally bold. Read at your own risk.

Avery point of view.

Mike looked at tattoo on my waist. His eyes filled with tears.

" Mike ? " I called.

" It... It... Must have hurted you. I am Cruel. I am monster " Mike said in tears and got up from me. He placed his hand on his forehead.

He started to cry. I got up and hold his hand. Mike looked at me in tears.

" It's not you. You didn't done this. The monster, which is already died in you " I said. Mike pulled me into a tight hug. He is just crying badly on my shoulders.

Small tears rolled in my eyes.

" I... Love you " Mike said.

" I love you too " I said. Mike broke the hug and looked at me. He slowly placed his finger on my lips.

He started to stare at my lips.

" Please... I want it tonight " Mike said in sad tone in tears. He came closer to my lips and he pulled my upper lip into his mouth.

He started to move his lips slowly. His soft lips touching my lips.

The kiss started to become passionate. Mike stopped. He took a breath. He kissed my forehead. He kissed my both cheeks. He slowly placed a kiss on my nose. He bent towards my neck. He moved my hair behind my ear. He pulled my ear nob.

Ah... It's... Just....

Weird feeling started in me. I don't know a moan escaped from my mouth. He keep on kissing my ear nob. When it's done. He slowly kissed my neck.

He hands are running around my back and grabbing my waist tightly.

He moved towards my throat. He started to place some kisses there. Suddenly he started to move his lips towards my cleavage. I gasped. Mike looked at me and made me lay on bed. He quickly got on me.

In a second his hands ran into my shirt while kissing me grabbed my breast.

I shivered.

It's disgusting.... It's awkward.

Mike looked at me in worried. I just smiled. He pulled my shirt up.

That's all. I placed my head down. I started to cover with my hands. Mike smiled.

" Look at me " Mike said. I looked at him.

" It's fine to be shy. It's fine to be awkward " Mike whispered slowly. He grabbed my lips. I just getting into him. I am trying my best to satisfy him.

I became more passionate and started to kiss him like a monster.

Mike stopped.

" Let's go slow " Mike said.

Idiot Avery.

His eyes started to roll around my upper body. He grabbed my waist and made me lift a bit. In a second he removed my bra.

I started to cover myself. Mike looked at me and smiled. He placed his hand on my head.

" Relax. Don't be nervous "

How can I not be nervous at this point ?

I nodded. He slowly removed my hands from covering. He explored my beasts.

He keep on staring at them.

That's embarrassing.

He bent down. He gave a look at me. He grabbed my left breast. I quickly closed my eyes.

He started to rub it.

Suddenly I felt his lips on my nipples. My opened my eyes quickly.

" Huh ? " I hold his head. He gave a look at me and started to lick it.

It's weird. What kind of stupid feeling is it ?

I frowen my eye brows.

When he is done with left. He grabbed the right. He is about to lick. I stopped him. Mike looked at me. He closed his eyes for a second.

Is he angry ?

" If... This goes on. I am sure we will not do it " Mike said seriously. I lowered my eyes.

Can't you let it go Avery. Why are you stopping such a romantic mood ?

He said. He rubbed my hair. He placed a small kiss on my lips. He continued what he left with.

He started to kiss my left breast. I just closed my eyes. Suddenly a moan escaped from my mouth.

I felt his lips on my stomach. He started to lick my stomach and kissing it. He moved towards my tattoo and placed a kiss on it. He again grabbed my lips. We started to kiss for a few minutes.

" Remove my shirt " suddenly Mike said while smiling.

" Huh ? " Mike took my hand and placed it on his buttons. He rolled his eyes towards the shirt.

I started to remove one by one. While Mike just placing small kisses on my breast.

In a second Mike removed his shirt. His 6 pack, His strong muscles, His tattoos around the body.

I placed my hand on his tattoos. Mike looked at me and grabbed my lips.

He keep on kissing me. Suddenly his hands reached on my xxxxx

I gasped. I made him stop.

Please.... Not touching such a sensitive part.

" Just look at me. " Mike said. He started to rub there.

Suddenly moans started escaping from my mouth.

Mike grabbed my pants and removed it. My eyes widen. Without a second he removed my panties.

No way.... It's disgusting.

I covered my eyes with my hands. Mike removed my hands and smiled.

" It's just us. " He said and placed a kiss on my forehead. Suddenly his hands reached there. In a second he inserted his finger in me.

" NO !!! " I yelled. Mike stopped quickly and looked at me in worried.

" Am I hard ? " He asked. I nodded as no. He smiled and continued doing that.

That's all moans started. He is doing it from past 5 minutes slowly.

Suddenly something wet came out.

Mike stopped. He looked down.

Don't say now he is going to lick it.

" I WON'T ALLOW IT " I shouted. Mike looked at me confused.

" What ? " Mike asked.

Mostly in porns they do that. Licking it.

" Aren't... You going.... To lick it ? " I asked hesitantly. Suddenly Mike laughed.

" Are you serious ? Do you want me to ? " Me asked while laughing. I nodded as no quickly.

Did I say something wrong ? This is what done right ?

He stopped laughing and came closer to my face.

" It's not porn. We are not doing sex here. We are doing love " Mike said. I blushed. He placed a kiss on my lips. He smiled.

" Now, Close your eyes " He said.

Huh ? But why ?

" Why ? " I asked.

" You will be panic. I am going to take it slow. Don't be scared " He said and smiled. I hold the blanket tightly and closed my eyes. I don't know what's happening.

There is a silence for few more minutes. It's just dark. Suddenly I felt something down.

Seriously ? Is he going to ?

I am about to move. Mike stopped.

" Don't move. " Mike ordered.

I am so scared that I started sweating.

It's going to pain. He already tried to do it.

Its damn pains so much.

" Shh... Relax " It's getting inside me slowly.

" Ah... " I whispered in pain. Mike pulled my hand and hold it tightly.

" Inhale... Exhale " Mike said. I didn't a second opened my eyes. I slowly started to take my breath and release it.

" AH.... " I yelled loudly. Tears dropped down my cheek.

He is completely in me. Mike hold my face.

I started to breath hardly.

How can somebody bare this much of pain ?

" Look at me " Mike said. I opened my teary eyes. I seen his face worried.

I looked down.

Blood.... I am bleeding.

" No, Don't look anywhere. Just look at me " Mike said making me see him.

" I.... Am bleeding " I said in tears.

" It's fine. It's fine " he said wiping my tears. He placed a kiss on my forehead. He hugged me.

" Don't cry. It's going to be fine. Let's enjoy this moment. I know it's pains. I will take slow. " He whispered in my ear. I nodded in tears. He looked at me.

He started to move slowly.

" Ah... " I whispered. Mike hold me tightly. He hugged me. We started to sweat.

He started to move slowly. I just controlling my pain as much as I can.

" Ah... " I yelled again. I quickly covered my mouth with my hand. Mike slowly removed my hand.

" It's... It's... Fine to shout " Mike said. He is having the same pain as I am going through.

Suddenly I don't know. We started to shake.

" Mike " I moaned in pain. Mike hugged me.

" Just... About to finish " He said in pain.

" AH.... " Mike yelled in pain. He stopped. We started to breath heavily.

I felt something got inside. I hold Mike tightly.

Mike relaxed on my shoulder.

" It's done " Mike said.

After a few minutes of relaxing. Mike looked at me and smiled. I blushed.

" Remove it. It's pains " I said and hit on his chest. He nodded and removed it slowly.

" Ah.... " I whispered.

" Ok ? " Mike asked. I nodded. He got of me and lay beside me. He pulled the blanket and covered us. I rested on his shoulder. Mike pulled me closer.

He started to stare at me.

" What ? " I blushed.

" seriously. How many times did you watched porns ? " Mike asked looking at me.

"You.... " I hit on his chest. We laughed. Mike pulled my hand. I blushed.

" Real life sex is not a porn. Got it ? " Mike said. I lowered my eyes tears rolled in my eyes.

" Hey... " He made me look at him.

" You are crying ? Idiot " Mike said and pulled me into a hug.

" I... Am sorry. I just want to let you know. That's it. " Mike said.

" It's not that " I said. Mike looked at me.

" Then ? "

" It's pains " I said sadly and pouted. Mike laughed.

" No pain. No gain " Mike said and pinched my nose. I smiled. We hugged so tightly.

I don't know what's the time. I don't know how much time we are in bed. I feel protected and comfortable in his arms and on this bed.

Seconds, minutes, hours passed.

Still we didn't parted. We are just hugging each other and talking about lots of things.

Mike point of view

She is beautiful. He is just mine. Only mine.

My wife. My only wife.

She is sleeping in my arms peacefully. I took her hand slowly and noticed that there is no ring on her hand.

Where is the ring Avery ? You really throwed it ?

It's fine. I am going to give you another most beautiful ring.

She is just so beautiful while she is sleeping. I placed a small kiss on her hair.

Suddenly my phone buzzed. I slowly removed my arm. Avery pulled her blanket and moved to another side. I smiled. I pulled my boxers and put in on.

I don't want to disturb her. I walked to balcony.

I quickly picked up the call. It's stefen.

" Don't you have manners ? Its a sin to disturb a lovely couple " I teased. There is a silence.

" Stefen ? Are you there ? " I asked.

It's completely silence again..

" M_ike.... " I heard stefen voice. He sounds sad.

" Are you okay ? " I asked in worried. Suddenly I heard him crying.

What happened ? Ana ? Did something happened to Ana ? Baby ?

" Ana, is fine right ? " I asked quickly.

" Ron.... Ron... " Stefen said sobs. My eyes widen.

" What happened to Pumpkin ? "

" Some gangsters kidnapped him " Stefen sobs.

" WHAT ? " I shouted.

That's the end.

After reading this chapter. I know the first thing clicks in mind.

" What ? Ron is kidnapped ? What's going to happen ? "

Wait for the next update.

I hope you guys like this episode. I struggled so much to write it. It's just beyond my other stories.

If you guys want me to upload next episode as soon as possible comment me. Let me know your views.

Please do share, like and comment.

When do you want me to upload next chapter ? Comment me.

More comments more quicker.

Thank you. Love you guys. ☐☐

kidnap

Mike point of view

" Mike... Please come to home. I... Will explain you everything " Stefen said in pain. I hung up the call.

Pumpkin kidnapped ? How can this happen ? Who would've done that ?

I am in shock. I quickly walked inside. There I seen Avery on bed in deep sleep. I walked to her slowly. I sat beside her. A tear rolled in my eyes.

You were so happy last night. If I let you know this incident. You will be panicked. I won't let that happen.

I have to go to stefen's house to know exactly what happened.

Without even a second. I slowly walked to dressing room. I got dressed. I gave a look at Avery again. And walked out of the room.

....

The minute I reached stefen's house. I got shocked to see that the whole house is just mess.

There are broken glass pieces every where and all things are just on ground.

I ran inside there I seen stefen and ana sat on sofa. They are crying.

The minute I looked at stefen. He got injured in several places. While ana got hurt on forehead.

" What.... Happened ? " I asked shockingly looking around. Stefen and ana looked at me. Ana came to me slowly and hugged me tightly.

She started crying in my arms.

" I... Am sorry Mike. I can't able to protect Ron. We tried our best " Ana cried. I broke the hug.

" What happened ? " I asked. Stefen came to me.

" We... Were having dinner. Suddenly some Gangsters around 5-6 people barged Into the house. They are holding guns. They hit me to death. They pushed ana on ground and pulled Ron and walked off " Stefen said in tears. My eyes widen in shock. I looked at ana bump.

Thank god !!! Baby is fine.

" I... Am sorry... We tried. But... Can able to save Ron " stefen said in tears.

" How.... Can I explain to Avery ? " I said. Tears rolled in my eyes.

" We.. have to say to her. She.... " Before ana say.

" NO !!!! I won't let her know. " I yelled.

" But.... " Before stefen continue.

" She was happy last night with me. I can't make her sad by saying this. Ron is her life. She treats him just like his son. I... Can't " I said. Stefen placed his hand on my shoulder.

" Mike, think. Is there any fights in business ? Do you doudt on anyone ? " Stefen asked.

Business fight ?

" Impossible. I never had any fights. Everyone used to be scared of me. How can anyone fight with me ? It's not about business " I said.

" Let's call the police " Ana said.

NO!!!!!

" No, if the kidnappers gets to know then.... they will do something to pumpkin " i said.

"Then, What we gone do ? mike. W e can't sit still " Stefen said.

" I will arrange a special team "I said and quickly pulled out my phone.

....

" I want all the details. I want him in tomorrow morning in my house " I said seriously and hung up the call.

" Do you think it's gone work ?" stefen asked.

" It has to work at any cost " I got up and about to leave.

" How are going to handle avery ?" Ana asked.

it's better not to tell her. Until tomorrow morning.

" i am not going to say to her " I said.

"if you go home now.The first thing she is going to ask is ron " Ana said.

" Will you guys help me ? " I asked looking at them. Stefen and ana looked at me confused.

Avery point of view.

My opened my eyes slowly. Sunlight hit on my eyes. I looked beside me.

Mike ? Where did he go ?

I gave a look at balcony.

I wrapped myself with blanket. The minute I got up. I seen the bed got dirty.

Avery..... The bed is full of stain.

I quickly pulled the blanket and ran into the washroom.

....

I looked around the house. I didn't find Mike anywhere.

Looks like he went to office.

How about making a call ? I quickly pulled my phone.

Number ? What is Mike's number ?

We never spoken on phone.

Now I have to wait till 8:00pm to see him.

Ron ? Ron is still with stefen. I have to give him a call.

His number is with me. I quickly made the call. After a few rings.

" Good morning stefen " I said. There is a complete silence on other side.

" Stefen ? Are you there ? " I asked.

" Ya, yes yes "

" I want to see Ron. Why don't you guys come home ? We can have lunch together " I said. There a second silence again.

" Avery..... Actually Ron want's to spend some time here. We will bring him tomorrow morning. " Stefen said.

Tomorrow ? But Ron can't live seeing me a day.

" But.... Is Ron okay ? He is not troubling you guys right ? Actually he can't live seeing me a day " I asked hesitantly.

" He... He... Is completely fine. He is just so adorable. He loves my place. " Stefen said.

" Oh !!! Then.... I won't worry. He is there ? I want to talk to him " I said.

A silence again. What's happening ?

" Ron.... Went out with Ana. When they come back I call you. " stefen said.

" It's fine. Make sure you call me when Ron is back " I said.

" Ya... Ya... "

" Avery... I am busy. I will call you later " Stefen said.

" Ya, Byee " I hung up the call.

When did Ron started being so close to them ?

Strange. As long he is happy. Let him stay. I don't have to be more possessive.

....

I looked at watch is mid night 9:00pm. I called stefen many times. But... There is no response. Mike is still not back to home.

I prepared dinner for him.

I walked to living room. I switched on the TV. Suddenly thunders started outside. Heavy wind, Windows started sounding. I quickly closed the windows.

Looks like it's going to rain heavily.

I sat on the sofa and started to watch tv.

There is a knock on the door.

Looks like Mike

I ran and quickly opened the door.

There I seen Mike stood. I smiled. He walked inside. He stared at me for a second. He pulled me into a hug.

Looks like he is tired.

" Are you tired ? " I asked. He just didn't respond to me and hugging me more.

He broke the hug and barley gave a smile.

Looks like he is so tired.

" Let's have dinner together " I said making a smile on my face.

" Let me get fresh up " Mike said before leaving me placed a small kiss on my forehead.

Is he so tired. He looks sad.

I stared at mike.

"Everything will be fine " I said. In a second he pulled me tightly.

What happened ?

"yes... Everything will be fine "He said sadly. Mike broke the hug suddenly i seen small tears are in his eyes.

"What happened?" I asked in worried tone. Mike quickly turned his face.

" Just....It's.... I left you just like that without saying to you. You should've called me " Mike said in sad tone. I lowered my head.

" I don't have your number " I said helplessly. Mike chuckled.

Good to see his smile on face.

Mike placed his hand on my head. I looked at him. He pulled his mobile from his jacket. He gave me the mobile.

" Add it " He said. I blushed.

"I will be back. Let's have dinner together " Mike said. I nodded.

Mike point of view

The minute i got into my room. I sat on bed numb.

Tears rolled in my face. I am trying my best to control it. I placed my hand on my head.

Ron.... Where are you my boy ?

I looked at the picture on table. It's avery and ron. I placed my hand on ron face. Tear dropped on the frame.

"I handled today. What about tomorrow ?" I said in tears. I cried silently for a minute. I placed the frame on it's place. I walked into the washroom.

....

I seen avery placed all the dishes on dinning table. I took a chair while avery sat beside me.

" Do you know, ron want's to be at stefen's house ? " Avery said taking a bite.

I am sorry......

"Really ? " I acted like i don't know.

" it's strange, Usually he won't stay without me " Avery said.

Did she got to know ?

" Let... Him be. He should learn about relationships " I said while eating. Avery nodded.

After we done eating.

I got seated on sofa.

Waiting for the call of inspector.

While Avery cleaning the kitchen, after she is done she came to me. She sat beside me. While I continuously waiting for call.

" Let me call Ron. I didn't spoke to him on morning " Avery said. My eyes widen in shock. She is about to pick up her mobile. I stopped.

Avery looked at me confused.

What I have to do ? What plan should I make again ?

Suddenly I started couching.

" Get... Me some water " I acted couching. Avery ran to kitchen.

Avery made me drink water. She started to tap my back slowly.

" Okay ? " I nodded.

She relaxed.

" You made me worry " Avery said. I smiled. She is about pick her mobile again.

I pulled her hand to me. Avery got shocked.

" Let's talk about last night " I diverted.

" Last night ? " She asked. I raised my eyebrow.

" Say it " I asked.

" What ? " She asked in confuse. I pulled her waist.

" Mike ? "

" Say it. I want to listen again " I asked.

" Say, what ? " She asked in confuse.

" I love you. Say it " I said looking into her eyes. She blushed placed her head down.

" Come on !!! I am waiting " I said. She nodded as no in shy. I quickly pulled her on my lap.

" Mike "

" Say it " I said coming closer to her lips.

" I LOVE YOU " She shouted. I smiled. She is blushing so much. Her cheeks turned red.

" I love you too " I said and placed a small kiss on her cheek.

" I... Won't do it again " Avery said and lowered her eyes.

" Do what ? " I asked.

"S.... ex " She blushed. I chuckled.

" It's not sex. It's love " I said and pulled her more closer.

" Whatever it is, let's not do it again " She said a little angrily.

" What ? Impossible. We are going to do it again " I said. Avery opened her mouth wide.

" No " She yelled. My smile faded.

Don't know where the anger got into me. I looked at her angrily.

Avery got scared by my looks. She quickly lowered her eyes.

" It... Pains.... Badly " Avery said. Suddenly her eyes filled with tears.

" I am just..... " I smiled and pulled her into hug. She started crying.

" I handled you last night. Are you still scared ? " I said sadly.

" I... Am just kidding. Why do you looked at me like that ? It makes me think of old Mike " She said in tears just like a small baby in my arms. I smiled.

" Sorry, I am just so tired today. I am waiting for a important call. When you said you won't do it. I got angry. I won't become that old myself show to you again " I said.

Ron's kidnap anger I am showing in front of Avery.

Suddenly my phone started to buzz. We broke the hug.

It's inspector.

" Let me take the call. Don't cry " I said wiped her tears and gave a small kiss on her forehead. She got off me.

I walked out of the house.

I quickly picked up the call.

" Yes " I said.

" Sir, we got to know the address. But... The major thing is why he kidnapped Ron ? " He asked.

" That's what I can't able to get ? " I asked.

" Let's go now " I said.

" No sir. We can't just go like that. It will be harmful for Ron "

" Then, what's the plan ? " I asked.

We started to discuss the plan.

After few minutes. I hung up the call. I got inside. There I seen Avery slept on sofa. I walked to her. Suddenly my phone buzz.

Unknown number.

I picked up quickly.

" Oh !!!! Mr. Perfect " I heard on other side.

Kidnapper.

My eyes widen in shock. I walked to balcony.

" Where is Ron ? " I asked angrily.

" That's a good guess. He is fine. He is just sleeping. I gave him some injections "

" WHAT ? Injections ? What are you doing to that small kid ? If you want money, Say it. I am ready to give you money " I said angrily. I hold my fist tightly. I heard a laugh on other side.

" Money ? I don't want money " He said.

He don't want money.

" I want your wife " He said. My eyes widen in shock. I hold my fist tightly.

" BASTARD !!!! WHO ARE YOU ? " I yelled angrily. My eyes turned red.

" Your wife knows me better " He said. My eyes widen in shock.

Avery knows him. That's strange.

" Where is Ron ? " Suddenly I heard a voice from behind. My eyes widen in shock.

I know it's Avery.

I hung up the call and turned around. There I seen Avery stood there in shock. I smiled.

" It's Ron. He wants to come " I said moving closer to her. Suddenly Avery moved back.

" I.... Heard everything. Where is Ron ? " She asked. Tears already appeared in her eyes.

" Avery.... Listen to me " I said and about to take her hand. She moved back.

" What happened to him ? " She asked.

I can't hide more than this.

" Let's.... Get seated first " I said and about to take her hand. She moved back. She walked out of the balcony.

" Avery " I called. I ran behind her. I quickly pulled her hand. She looked at me in tears.

" I will go to stefen's house. I will bring Ron back " She said angrily.

" Avery, calm down. " I said.

" LEAVE MY HAND !!! " She yelled angrily. I slowly released her hand. She is about to go to main door. I made her stop.

" Listen to me " I said.

" WHERE IS RON ? " She shouted angrily in tears.

" Ron.... Is.... Kidnapped " I said. That's all. She took a step back. She got numb.

" Avery. I know where is pumpkin. We informed a special team. We already planned everything " I am trying to make her calm.

" I will find Ron myself " She said about to open door. I stopped.

" It's raining. Where are you going to find him ? We planned. We will find Ron tomorrow " I said. She angrily removed my hands from her shoulder.

" He is my life. He is my everything. He gets cold easily. He can't live without me. " Avery started to say in tears. Suddenly she started to cry.

I took her face in my hands.

" He will be fine. I promise, I will bring him to you safe " I said. She just keep on crying.

plan

Mike point of view

We are discussing how to go with the plan.

" Let's go they are waiting for us " Stefen said.

I nodded. I quickly pulled my jacket.

" I am coming too " Suddenly we heard Avery voice. As we turned around there I seen her walking downstairs. Ana is behind her.

Stefen looked at me and quickly gave me a signal as no.

I walked to Avery.

" I promise. I will bring back Ron " I said and hold her face in my hands.

" I will come with you " Avery said.

You don't know they are gangsters Avery.

He told me that he knows you. He wants you. I can't take the risk.

" Listen to me.... " Before I complete. She removed my hands.

" I am coming that's final " She said angrily. I looked at Ana to handle it. Ana walked to Avery placed hand on her shoulder.

" Avery, Mike will bring Ron back. Trust him. Let's wait at home. " Ana said. Avery nodded as no.

" I am going to see Ron first. I have to see he is fine. " Avery said.

She is making things complicate.

" You are staying here. That's all " I said angrily.

" Fine. I will find him myself " Avery said and about to go.

" Why are you making things complicated ? " I shouted angrily. She turned to me. I seen tears in her eyes.

" Ron.... Is kidnapped. It's been 24 hours. Do you think I am making things complicate ? Ron Is my life. He is just 5 years old. Everyone is using him. You used Ron for gaining me. Now this kidnapper too took Ron..... " Avery said in tears.

My eyes widen in shock. She is right. Every single thing she said is right.

I just placed my head down. Tear rolled in my eyes.

" What he wants ? " Avery asked angrily in tears.

He wants you. I won't let that happen. I won't give you to anybody. Even Ron's life in danger. I will protect you first.

I love pumpkin. I love him. But more than him. I love you.

You two are my family. I won't let anything happen. If he is your life than I will do whatever it takes to protect pumpkin.

" Avery, Mike is doing his best to save ron. Trust him. " Stefen said.

" I trust him. I didn't say that I don't trust him. I just want ron. I want to see him first. Let me come with you " Avery said in tears. I walked to Avery. I controlled my tears. I slowly wiped her tears with my thumb.

" Fine. Come with us " I said.

" But Mike... " Before stefen speaks. I gave him a look. He looked at me worried.

" Promise me that you will not take a step outside the car. When I find Ron. I will bring him straight to you. Ok ? "

Avery nodded quickly. I smiled.

" I want to come too " Ana said.

" WHAT ? No way " Stefen said angrily.

" Let her come too " I said. Ana smiled.   Stefen looked at me angrily.

" We are not going for a pinic. She is pregnant. Do you get that ? Pregnant " Stefen repeated.

" Mike, No. It's not good for Ana to come " Avery said.

" Exactly " Stefen yelled.

" You will be bored. Let Ana accompany you. " I said.

" I am good at accompany " Ana said in excitement.

" Are you guys insane ? I won't let her come with us. She is 8 months pregnant. Look at her bump " Stefen said angrily pointing to her stomach.

" They are going to stay in car. I will let a Bodyguard stay with them " I said. Stefen looked at me angrily.

" Let's go. It's going to be late " I said.

" But... " Before stefen complete.

" Stefen " I looked at him angrily. He just walked out angrily.

....

We reached the place it's outskirts.

Not even single people are visible there.

Except me, Ron and Avery, ana and one Bodyguard.

" Like promised.... " Before I continue.

" Don't step out " Avery completed. I smiled and gave a kiss on her forehead.

I wish my plan works. I will never let him get you.

I don't know why he wants you. What's your relationship with him ? But... I won't let him get you.

" If you step out. I am going to kill you " Stefen said angrily. Me and Avery smiled.

" I won't. " Ana said.

" That's better " Stefen said.

" Let's go " I said. We walked out.

" Mike, you know it's dangerous to keep them here " Stefen said angrily.

" It's not the kidnappers place " I said.

" WHAT ? " Stefen shouted.

" Do you think, I am going to let them come with us that easily ? We are going to take another car. Let's go " I said.

" Wow !!!! You plan is just... "

" Let's go " I said.

" Watch them " I said to Bodyguard. He nodded.

We walked from there.

....

The minute we reached the place.

I quickly pulled out the gun and started to load the bullets.

" You... Know how to shoot ? " Stefen shocked. I nodded.

" I am National campaign " I said and quickly arranged everything.

" Hold it " I said and gave a gun to stefen. His hands started to shake.

" I.... Am a doctor. I.... Treat people not kill them " stefen said Shivering. I chuckled.

" I didn't gave to kill anybody. It's just for safety "

Stefen exhaled the breath.

" Are you going to kill too ? Did police gave permission to you ? " Stefen asked.

" I won't let it use. If it's necessary I must use it. Even if it's against law " I said.

A car stopped in front of us.

Team got out.

" Are you guys ready ? " I said. They nodded.

" Mike, don't use it until if someone tries to harm you " Inspector said pointing to gun. I nodded.

" I don't think you guys needed. We will handle it " Inspector said.

" I have to make sure Ron is fine " I said. Inspector nodded.

We walked into the building.

It's just old wooden house.

Team walked forward holding guns in there hands.

" Do you think this gangster is smarter ? " Stefen whispered slowly.

" He is " I said. We walked inside. We found two people standing in front of a room. He quickly hided.

Team walked forward before they take guns to shoot us. Team shooted them.

It's sound proof guns.

We walked slowly. Inspector pointed one member to open the door. The minute we opened the door.

My eyes widen in shock only to find pumpkin there.

He is tied up with Ropes. A tape is on his mouth. He is unconscious lying there on ground.

" Pumpkin " I whispered. I am about to go. Inspector stopped me. He nodded as no.

A tear rolled in my eyes seeing him in that state.

Inspector bent down only to find a wire which is connected to a bomb.

" Don't step on it. It's gets blast " He warned. We nodded. Inspector slowly took a step without stepping on it. He walked to ron and quickly removed all the ropes. He again slowly walked to us.

Thank god !!!!

The minute inspector gave Ron into my arms. I looked at his cute little face. His face is dull and pale.

" Take him to hospital. You guys get out " Inspector said.

" Stefen take him hospital. I am going to find the kidnapper " I whispered.

" Are you stupid ? Are you guys going to take your life's on risk. He is a gangster not a normal mam. Get out " Inspector said angrily.

" He is right. Let's go Mike. They will find him " Stefen said. I nodded and quickly got up and

We nodded. Me and stefen walked out.

We started to run and run.

Finally we reached to our car.

" Stefen. Start the engine " I shouted. He nodded. We both got seated. In a second we drove off.

The minute we reached.

I found Avery and ana in car. The minute they seen us. They about to open the door.

" NO !!! " I shouted. I ran and we quickly got seated. The body guard drove in a second.

" HOSPITAL !!! RIGHT NOW " I shouted. Ron is in my arms still like a dead body.

" Not hospital. To my personal clinic. I will inform my friend to come there. He will check ron. " Stefen said.

Yes, the gangsters is not caught yet.

While I seen Avery in shock. I took her hand.

" He is fine. He is just unconscious " I said breathing heavily.

Tears are in her eyes.

" R.... On... Why... He is unconscious ? " Avery barley spoke. She is continuously looking at Ron not taking him in her arms.

" He is fine Avery. We are taking him to hospital right ? " Stefen said.

" Yes, don't worry " Ana said.

Avery let out a cry. She started crying.

With one hand. I pulled Avery to my chest.

" Don't cry " I said.

Tear rolled in my eyes. I looked at Ron's face. He is just like a dead body in my arms.

Get up pumpkin.

....

The minute we reached the stefen's clinic. He got down quickly. I hold Ron tightly and ran Into the house.

While they followed me.

Stefen's friend is already got here. I quickly placed him on bed.

The minute he looked at Ron.

" Let him get air. Please go out " he said. Avery quickly nodded as no.

" I won't " I gave a signal to start check up. He nodded. While ana and stefen walked out.

I hold Avery tightly. She is crying continuosly.

" Shh.... " I started to tap her hair. She is not even looking at Ron. She buried her head Into my chest. Doctor looked at me worried. I frown my eye brows.

" He is fine. But.... " He stopped. While Avery just can't able to listen all this. She hold my shirt tightly.

I shook my head to don't say. He nodded.

" He need to rest " He said. I closed my eyes for a second. I relaxed. Avery in a second she turned and ran to Ron.

While doctor pointed me to come outside. I walked behind him.

Ana and stefen stood up seeing us.

" He is fine right ? " Ana asked quickly.

He looked worried.

" James. Split out " stefen said.

" He was poisoned with injections " He said.

We got shocked.

Yes, That bastard told that he injected some injections.

" Is it dangerous ? " I asked quickly.

" No, I gave him a antidode. He will be fine. But.... " He stopped again.

" But ? " I asked.

" The poison injection effected his lungs. He.. will be having breathing problem " He said.

" Poison ? " Suddenly we heard a voice. There Avery stood in shock. I ran to her.

" Avery "

She ran outside. I ran behind her. I pulled her hand.

" Where are you going ? " I asked. She looked at me in tears.

" They... Poisoned him " She said in tears.

" He is fine " I said.

" The 5 years little boy..... Suffers from breathing " She said while crying. I pulled her tightly.

I controlled my tears. I pressed my lips tightly.

" We will handle him. We both are here for pumpkin. He will be fine " I said.

" Look at me " I said and broke the hug. I lifted her chin and placed a small kiss on her lips. She started to cry on my lips.

" No.... No... " I said and started to place kiss on her lips again.

I can't able to control my tears.

I started crying too.

" No... Please " I said in tears. She just crying so badly placing he head down. I placed another kiss on lips again.

" Don't... I can't see you like this. I promised myself that I won't let you cry. " I started to wipe her tears.

" Please " I requested. She is in so much pain. I can't able to handle her. I looked up.

To stop myself tears to drop. Her sobs making me remember the days I made her cry like this.

" Avery.... " I whispered. She is sobbing.

God !!! Help me to let her stop crying.

I pulled her tightly. I kissed her temple. She hold me so tightly.

She is crying the minute she seen Ron in car. She still didn't stopped.

I never cried like this. Why i am crying just like a baby too ?

" If you don't stopped crying. I am not going to talk to you " I warned angrily. She broke the hug and looked at me.

" You're making me cry more " She said and started sobbing again. I laughed. She stopped crying. I placed a small kiss on her lips. I started to explore her face which is now mess.

I removed her hair locks behind her ear and wiped her tears.

" You cried too " Avery said. I quickly wiped my tears.

" No " I said.

" You did " Avery said and smiled.

" So, what ? I already cried in front of you " Avery laughed.

" Then, why are you embrassed ? " Avery asked while smiling. I smiled.

" Who is embrassed ? " I said.

I am blushing.

Suddenly my phone begin to buzz.

I placed a kiss on Avery forehead.

" Get inside " I said. She nodded and walked off. I quickly picked up the call.

" Mike, We found the kidnapper " Inspector said.

Damon

Mike point of view

I barged into the room angrily. I seen a man sat in front of inspector.

I didn't seen him clearly every single part of my body wants me to kill him.

I ran to him and gave a hard punch on his face. In a second blood came out from his mouth.

" Mike, calm down " Inspector tried to stop me. I punched him again and pulled his collar.

" BASTARD !!!! " I yelled angrily and about to punch him again.

" Leave... Me sir... Please " He requested. I looked at him angrily.

" You kidnapped a kid and warned me. What do you know about my wife ? Split it " I said angrily and pulled his collar angrily. He started to shiver.

" I... I... Didn't kidnapped your child " He said while Shivering.

" WHAT ? " I am about to punch him.

"Mike, Listen to him " Inspector said and pulled me away from him.

" I... Just work for him. I didn't kidnapped anybody " He said in fear. I am now out of control. I went to him and punched on his face again.

" Mike " Inspector stopped me.

" WHERE IS HE ? WHERE IS THE BASTARD ? " I yelled angrily.

" I... Just done for money. I didn't seen him. " He said. I can't able to control my anger.

I thought he got caught. He is more genius. What he plans to do ?

" Mike, calm down. We will find him. " Inspector said.

" He wants my wife. How dare he says that ? I don't know what he will do next ? Please find him inspector " I said. He nodded.

" You... " I went to that bastard and punched again.

" Say it. Where he lives ? What's his plan ? Why he want my wife ? " I asked angrily.

" I... Don't know anything sir. I just kidnapped your son because he told me to do. I just want money. So..... " Before he speak further. I walked out of the room. While inspector followed me.

" He is saying lies. He might be not saying truth to us. May be he is the kidnapper " I said.

" No Mike, He is right. He is not the Kidnapper. I checked his background, he is just from a normal family. The actual culprit is not caught yet. Your family has to be careful. I will arrange few police at your house. " He said. I just nodded.

....

The minute I reached home. Avery came to me.

" Is culprit got caught ? " She asked quickly. I looked at her worried face.

No, I can't make her worry. I have to lie to her.

" Yes " I said and made a smile on my face.

" Really ? But... Why they are lots of police outside of our home ? " Avery asked.

" It's... For safety. I can't take risk. Let them stay for few days " I said. Avery nodded. She is above to go and turned again to me.

" Why did he Kidnapped Ron ? " She asked in worried. I took her hands slowly.

" Just for money. From now on you and Ron not going to take a step out. Got it ? " I said.

" He got arrested right ? Then... " Before she continue.

" Please.... Listen to me. Just for me. Don't take step out. Till I say " I warned. Avery looked at me confused and nodded. I pulled her into a tight hug.

I won't let anything happen to you nor Ron.

I wont let you guys out of my sight.

" Where is pumpkin ? " I asked and broke the hug.

" He is still unconscious. " Avery said sadly. I placed my thumb on her cheek.

" He will be conscious at any time " I said. Avery nodded. Suddenly my phone buzzed.

Unknown number ?

I looked at Avery.

" Let me take the call " I said and walked to balcony and quickly closed the window.

I picked up the call.

" Oh !!! You missed " He said on other side. I hold my fist tightly in anger.

" Do you think by saving that kid can change ? You can't able to catch me " He said.

" You can't able to get what you want " I said angrily. He laughed loudly.

" I will " He said angrily. I can't able to control my anger.

" Let's fight.Let's finish this stupid game you are playing " I said and chuckled.

" Game ? I still not yet started " He said.

" By the way. How is my lovely Avery ? " He asked.

My eyes widen in anger. I just want to throw the phone.

" She still remembers me. " He said.

What's between Avery and him. He must be danger. He knows everything about Avery.

" If you want to fight, show yourself. Don't hide like a cat " I said angrily.

" Hiding ? Avery knows me better. Just tell her my name. Look how she reacts " He said. I got confused.

What happened between them that Avery gets scared just by his name.

" Damon, Damon Salvatore " He just said that and hung up the call.

Damon Salvatore ?

....

" RON !!! " Suddenly I heard a scream. I quickly ran upstairs.

I found Ron on bed struggling for breathing. While Avery crying holding Ron in her arms. I ran to them and quickly pulled the oxygen mask and placed it on Ron's nose.

Ron got controlled. I let out a breath.

I placed Ron on bed. He opened his little eyes slowly. I seen Avery crying silently. I hold her hand.

" Don't cry in front of him. He is scared. " I whispered slowly. Avery wiped her tears quickly.

" Si...s " Pumpkin barley spoke. Avery quickly took his little hand.

" Yes, I am here. Just sleep " Avery said and made a smile on her face. Ron eyes moved towards me.

" Super... Man " Ron said. I placed my hand on his head.

" We are here. " I said.

" When... I am going to play ? I don't remember anything. Am I sick ? " He said. Avery trying her best to control tears.

" No, You are just weak. When you get better let's play together. Ok " I said. A small tear rolled in my eyes.

" Super... Man " Pumpkin called. I raised my eye brows.

" Shh... No more talking. Sleep, when you get up. We will play together " I said and made a smile. While I seen Avery ran out of the room. Ron smiled a little from his oxygen mask.

She can't able to control her tears.

I covered him with the blanket while ron closed his eyes. I quickly walked outside. There i seen Avery crying badly.

I ran to her and pulled her into tight hug.

" I... Can't see him like this " She cried in my arms.

" He will be fine " I said tapping her head.

I won't let him get you. I won't let you cry. ....

Do avery really knows Damon Salvatore ?

Do avery really gets scared of his name ?

I have to know him. I have to know what happened between them. So, it will be easier for me to find him.

I walked towards the kitchen where Avery is cooking. She is chopping vegetables. She looked at me and smiled.

" What happened ? " She asked. While I just keep on staring at her.

How should I ask her ?

I walked to her and wrapped my arms around her waist and rested my head on her neck. Avery blushed.

" Ana's due date is tomorrow. I am so excited to see her baby " Avery said while chopping.

" Hmm " I placed a small kiss on her neck. She shivered.

" Mike " She started to blush. I pulled her to me. I stare at her face and moved her hair locks behind her ear.

" What happened ? " Avery asked.

I can't lose you Avery. I won't let him get you. I changed myself for you.

My PYSCO, My arrogance, My anger, My habits. I changed every single thing for you.

I love you Avery. I love you so much that I can't lose you. I dreamed of a family which I have right now in front of me. I can't lose it.

" Mike ? " Avery called. I came out of my thoughts. I quickly lifted her and placed her on kitchen platform.

" Hey, We are in kitchen " Avery blushed. I chuckled. She is so short that I can reach her easily. I quickly pulled her lips for a second.

" I love you" I said. Avery blushed placing her head down. She is about to get down. I stopped her.

" Mike, I have to cook " Avery said.

Come on ask Mike.

" I have something to ask you " I said. She raised her eyebrows.

" What is it ? " She said coming closer to my face. I seen smile on her face. She looks so happy.

Come on !!!! Mike ask her.

" Do... You know.... " I started to ask hesitantly. She is eagerly waiting for my question.

" What ? " She asked placing her hand on my cheek.

No, I won't. I can't do it. I can't make her sad.

" Nothing " I said and placed my head down. Avery wrapped her arms around my neck.

" Every thing is going to be fine " She said. I raised my head only to see her happy face.

" How do you get to know that I am sad ? " I asked while smiling.

" I know " She said. I smiled. I made her get down. She started preparing food again.

Avery point of view

I am done with preparing dinner. I looked around I didn't find Mike anywhere.

Where did he go ? Is he upstairs ?

Ahhh.... His house is so big that I can't know where is he ?

" I am here " I heard his voice. I turned around only to find Mike holding Ron in his hands. Ron looks happy and smiling at me.

My eyes widen in shock. Ron is fine ? He got conscious.

I ran to them and pulled Ron into my arms. I placed kiss all over his face.

" You are fine. " tears rolled in my eyes. I smiled and cried too seeing him so happy.

" Sis, I am hungry " Ron said. Me and Mike smiled.

" I made lots of dishes " I said.

....

After we are done eating dinner. I seen ron and Mike playing.

I walked to them and I got seated beside Mike.

" Are you happy ? " Mike asked. I nodded and rested my head on his shoulder while Mike seated on Mike's lap.

" Uncle, let's play another game. I am going to run you are going to catch me " Ron said. I quickly Lifted my head from Mike's shoulder.

" NO !!! " Me and Mike said at once. Ron made a sad face.

" Why ? " He asked. Me and Mike looked at each other sadly. Mike pulled Ron closer.

" Pumpkin, Listen to me. You are sick. From now on you are not going to run fastly nor jump hardly nor do anything with makes you get hard to breath ok ? " Mike said. Ron nodded

" What are we going to play then ? " Ron asked. Mike started to think. I smiled.

" How about a movie ? " Mike said.

Movie ? Mike never watched a movie. He don't know any movies too.

" YEHHHH !!!!! " Ron shouted. Suddenly Ron started to cough. Mike quickly tapped his back.

" When you feel that you can't breath. Breath in, breath out. Got it ? " Mike said. Ron done the same.

" Good boy " Mike smiled.

" Thank you " I whispered to Mike. He looked at me.

" He is my family too " Mike said. I smiled.

" Where are we going to watch movie ? " I asked. Mike got up holding Ron. He gave me his hand.

" Let's go " He said. I looked at his hand.

" Where ? " I asked and smiled.

" You will know " Mike said. I took his hand. We walked to the lift.

" Are we going upstairs ? " I asked. Mike nodded. We got inside. Mike quickly pressed the top floor button.

Why he is taking us there ?

He is taking us to the same room where he did all his PYSCO things. We got out of the lift. I quickly stopped Mike. I nodded as no in fear. Mike placed Ron on floor. He took my face in his hand.

" I promise. I won't hurt you " He said looking into my eyes. Tears appeared in my eyes.

" No, I won't let you go into that room again " I said in sad tone. Mike laughed.

" Come with me " Mike about to take me Into the room. I got scared and just stood there in fear. In a second Mike lifted me into his arms.

" Mike "

" Shh.... Close your eyes " He ordered. I furrow my eyebrows. While ron started to laugh.

" Sis is in uncle's arms " Ron laughed.

Ron you don't know what is inside.

" Close your eyes " He said again. I nodded as no. Mike about to come closer to my lips. I quickly closed my eyes tightly. I heard the door opened and Mike placed me on floor.

" Open your eyes " Mike whispered in my ear. I hold my hand tightly in fear.

" Avery " Mike called and quickly pinned my cheek hardly.

" MIKE " I yelled in pain and quickly opened my eyes. Mike gave me a signal to watch around. I turned around.

I am shocked to see the room is completely changed. There is no scary pictures, no tattoo Machines.

The walls are painted with pink color and the huge digital screen is on the wall and in front of it sofas are being placed and behind the sofa there is a huge bed. I turned to see the washroom is constructed there too.

" Do you like it ? " Mike came closer to me. I literally had tears in my eyes.

" Hey, Crying again " Mike said wiping my tears.

" How do you know I am scared of this room ? " I asked in tears.

" When you got drunk. You spiled out. I thought of renovating It. What do you think ? Do you like this movie theatre ? " Mike asked. I nodded in tears.

" Sis, Huge screen. Are we going to watch movie here ? " Ron asked and got seated on sofa quickly with his toy in his hand.

" Yes " Mike said and took my hand and we got seated.

" Who gone decide the movie ? " I asked. Mike started to rub his neck in awkward.

" I don't watch movies. " He said. I chuckled.

" I know. When I person can't select a favorite food, how he is going to select a movie " I said.

" I am going to select " Ron raised his cute little hand.

" What is it ? " I asked.

" Do... Do... " Ron started to pronounce.

I know you like doraemon.

" It's doraemon Ron. How many times I told his name still your pronounce it wrong ? " I said.

" Doraemon ? Is it romantic movie ? " Mike asked quickly. I hit his chest.

" Ouch !!! "

" It's cartoon " I said angrily.

" Let's watch romantic movie without Ron sometime " Mike whispered.

" You.... " I am about to beat him.

" Sis, play it " Ron said. I searched it and it started to play.

" Yeh.... Do... Do.... "

Here Ron goes again.

" Doraemon " I corrected.

Mike pulled me closer. I blushed. We started to watch.

After a few minutes I seen Ron sleeping on Mike's lap. I am about to wake him up.

" Let him sleep " Mike said.

" But... Your leg will get numb " I said.

" It's fine. " Mike said. Suddenly Ron whispered in his sleep.

" Do... Do.... "

We laughed slowly.

" Doraemon " Mike whispered in Ron's ear. We smiled looking at Ron.

" Yeah.... DAMON " Ron yelled.

Hearing the name. My eyes widen in shock. I shivered in a second.

" DAMON.... DAMON " Ron started to yell loudly. I got numb.

I started shivering and sweating. I can't able to hear any sound in the room.

" Avery... Avery.... " Mike voice turned low.

Don't just be a silent readers. Comment me so, that I know how you guys like my book. I seen most people are not responding to my book. I want to stop writing. When people don't encourage being a writer it's gets disappointed.

Please do like, Share,comment.

I will kill him

Mike point of view

The minute she heard Damon from Ron's mouth. She started to shiver.

I slowly placed Ron of sofa. I hold Avery face in my hands.

" Avery... What happened ? " I asked looking into her eyes.

She just shivering. In a second she ran out of the room.

Damon ? He said hearing his name will let Avery scare.

What happened between them ? What he did with Avery ?

I lifted Ron in my arms and placed him on bed. I quickly ran out of the room. I started to look around. I didn't find her anywhere.

I seen the lift it's showing downstairs.

I quickly took stairs. I started to ran ran. I looked at lift again. I stopped at first floor.

Where she is going ? It's dangerous outside.

I quickly pulled out my phone.

" STOP AVERY !!! " I yelled at staff. I ran downstairs.

There I seen her stopped by my guards. I am out of breath. I ran to her. I gave signal to guards to disperse.

" Avery... Avery... " I hold her shoulders. She just not in her sense. I can only see tears in her eyes.

" Let's get inside. " I said and pulled her wrist and took her Into the house.

The minute we reached Into our bedroom.

" What happened ? Why are you behaving like this ? " I asked in worried tone. She just not answering to me.

" AVERY !!! " I yelled in anger and pulled her shoulders.

What's happening to you ?

She looked at me.

" He... He... " She started to say in her sobs.

" Say it. I am listening " I said and Eagerly waiting for her response.

Say it Avery. Why are you so scared of him ?

" He... Touched... Me... Here " Avery said in her sobs showing her Breasts. My eyes widen in shock.

" W_ho ? " I asked angrily.

I know. I know, who it is. I want to hear from her.

" D... Da... Damon " She cried. I pulled her into a tight hug. She started to cry badly in my arms. I can't able to control my anger. My eyes filled with anger and small tears filled in my eyes.

" He.... Tried.... To rape me. He will get me Mike. He won't leave me. I am scared of him " Avery said hugging me tightly. My eyes widen in shock.

He tried to rape Avery. So, he want Avery body.

I broke the hug. I wiped her tears.

" No, I wont let him get you. " I said.

" I.... Heard his name after 2 years. I ran from him. He... Will find me Mike. He wants my body " Avery said in tears.

No, I won't tell her that he found Avery. If she knows she will be scared. I will handle that bastard.

" I won't let him get you. Look. You are in our home. You are safe. You are safe with me. Nobody can take you away from me. " I said.

" Don't leave me " Avery said in tears and hugged me tightly.

" Never " I said.

So, you want Avery. You want to have my wife. You tried to rape my wife.

I was confused for the meaning of kidnapping Ron. Now I got it.

I won't leave you bastard.

I am going to kill you. You made Avery suffer. Now, I will show you what's Mike Wilson do.

....

I hardly made her sleep. I placed a small kiss on her forehead. I am about to get up. She hold my hand tightly.

" Don't leave me " She whispered in her sleep. A tear rolled in my eyes. I slowly removed my hand.

I walked to balcony and pulled out my phone.

" Inspector, I know the reason behind why that bastard doing all this. He wants Avery. He will do anything to get Avery. Search him. I want that bastard in front of me " I said angrily holding my fist tightly.

" Mike, we will search him. We got some clues. I am sure we will find him. " Inspector said.

" I will kill him myself " I said and hung up the call. I am about to get inside. Suddenly my phone buzzed.

Stefen.

I picked up the call.

" Hey buddy, how it's going ? " Stefen said.

" I got know. Who is the kidnapper " I said angrily.

" What ? Who ? When ? How ? " Stefen got shocked.

" He wants Avery " I said holding my fist tightly in anger.

" WHAT ? Avery ? Why ? " He asked in confused.

" He tried to rape Avery. Now he wants to get her body " I said angrily.

" Are you serious ? He is gangster Mike. How are you going to face it ? " He asked shockingly.

" Don't know. What I know right now is that I will kill him " I said angrily.

" Let police handle it. It's better not to let Avery and Ron come out. " He warned.

Ana, is ana fine. Avery said she is going to deliver soon.

" Stefen, How is Ana ? When is her due date ? " I asked.

" It's tomorrow. Don't worry about us. We will fine. Just take care of Avery and Ron " Stefen said.

" I arranged bodyguards around your home. They follow you every where " I said.

" Mike, We don't need it. "

" I can't take risk stefen. Just listen to me " I warned.

" Fine. Fine " stefen said. I hung up the call.

Avery point of view

" No !!! " I yelled while waking up.

" Hey, I am here " In a second Mike pulled me into a tight hug.

" It's me. It's me " I said tapping my hair. I felt relief in his arms. I just closed my eyes.

" What's the time ? " I asked sleepy. He slowly rubbed my hair and pulled me closer.

" It's 1:00pm " He said and placed a kiss on my temple.

Ron ? Is he still sleeping in theatre room ?

" Mike, Ron... " Before I complete.

" I made him sleep in his room " He said. I smiled.

I didn't told him the entire truth about Damon.

" Avery " Mike called. I broke the hug and looked at him.

" You don't need to be scared of anything. I won't let anything happen to you " He said. A tear rolled in my eyes.

I am relief that bastard Damon is not behind me. Mike can't defeat him. He can do anything to get me.

" Hmm " I smiled in tears. Mike took my hand and about to interlink our fingers.

" Did you really thrown our wedding ring ? " Mike asked in sad tone. My eyes widen.

Shut !!! I literally forgot about our wedding ring. Yes, I throwed it. But... When I found it. I hide it safety.

I quickly got up.

" Where are you going ? " Mike asked quickly.

I ran towards my cupboard and opened my safe box and quickly pulled out the ring. I smiled. I turned to Mike and showed him the ring.

His face turned into a bright smile.

" You didn't thrown it " Mike ran to me and hugged me tightly.

" You said, you thrown it " Mike asked quickly.

" When did I say ? " I asked in confused. Mike broke the hug.

" When you were drunk " Mike pinched my nose.

Did I say it ? Idiot Avery.

" Ouch !!! " I whispered in pain. Mike smiled.

" Put on " I said. Mike looked at me confused. I showed him the ring. He smiled and took the ring from my hand and slowly inserted on my finger. I smiled.

" Don't ever remove it again " Mike warned.

" Yes boss " I saluted him. He pulled my hand. Mike came closer to my lips and about to kiss. Suddenly I felt like vomit. I quickly placed my hand on my mouth and ran into washroom.

I started to vomit.

Mike point of view

She ran into the washroom.

" Avery " I walked behind her. I got shocked to see Avery vomiting badly. I rubbed her back. She done vomiting. I quickly took the tissue and placed it on her mouth.

" Are you okay ? " I asked in worried tone. She look pale. She rested her head on my chest.

" What happened ? " I asked in worried tone.

" Don't know " She said sadly.

" Let me call the doctor " I said and about to leave. Avery pulled my hand.

" Please... Stay with me. I am scared tonight " She said sadly. I hold her face in my hands.

" But... You need doctor " I said.

" Let's call tomorrow. It's past mid night " She said in low tone.

" But... " Before I complete.

" They have family too. It's not good to call someone this late " She said.

" Are you okay now ? " I asked in worried tone.

" Hmm "

I pulled her into a tight hug.

I took her to bed made her sit on bed. I got on kneels and took her hand.

" What happened ? " I asked in worried tone.

" I don't know. I felt like vomiting. " She said in low tone. I placed my hand on her cheek.

" Take rest " I said and made her lay on bed. I got beside her. I pulled her close to me and closed my eyes.

" Avery " I called while I closed my eyes.

" Hmm "

" Are you asleep ? " I asked.

" No " she said and hugged me tightly. I pulled her closer.

" Can I ask.... About... The incident happened in theatre room ? " I asked hesitantly. Avery pressed my shirt tightly. I opened my eyes. I placed my hand on her palm.

" It's ok. I won't ask " I said and removed her hair locks behind her ear.

" Mike, Ron's wants a puppy " Avery said. She just closed her eyes and just so relaxed in my arms.

Yes, I heard them talking about dogs. Ron want's a puppy.

" Puppy ? " I said like I don't know about it.

" Yes, can we adopt a puppy for Ron ? " Avery asked while sleeping.

" No "

Avery opened her eyes quickly. She lifted her head and looked at me sadly.

" Why? " She asked.

" I don't like dogs " I said and pulled her head on my chest.

" You don't like anything. You don't have favourite food. You don't have any likes or dislikes, you like black colour. " Avery said a little angrily. I smiled.

" I always been like this " I said.

" Do you have dream ? Or it is also not there in your dictionary " She asked a little angrily.

Ofcourse my dream is having a family finally he became true.

I remained silent.

She sighed.

" Your dream must be get ride of your PYSCO. Am I right ? " She asked. I smiled. I nodded as no.

" Then.... " Before she speak. I placed a kiss on her lips. After a few minutes I started to move my lips. I started to kiss her lower lip. I closed my eyes and just pulled her closer to me and started to kiss her slowly. Avery got still. After a long kiss. I parted and looked into her eyes.

" The family " I said. She blushed.

We slept peacefully pulled closer to eachother.

....

I woke up when I heard my phone buzz. I seen Avery sleeping peacefully. I quickly pulled my phone and walked to balcony.

Stefen.

" Yes " I said in sleepy.

" MIKE... " He yelled.

" Ouch !!! " I ear pained.

" Can't you speak slowly ? " I said a little angrily.

" MIKE..... ANA IS BLESSED WITH CUTE BOY " He yelled again.

My eyes widen. A smiled appeared in my eyes.

" Congratulations father " I said.

" Don't let Avery come here. It's dangerous. Don't inform her that Avery delivered. She don't know the truth that kidnapper is not caught yet. She insists of coming here " Stefen said.

" I will not inform her " I said. I hung up the call.

" MIKE !!!! " Suddenly I heard a loud scream. My eyes widen. I ran into the room only to find Avery stood of bed. She got down and ran to me and hugged me tightly. She is so happy and smiling brightly.

What happened ?

" Mike, Ana gave birth to a boy " She said. My eyes widen in shock.

How Avery knows ?

I broke the hug. She looks so happy and smiling brightly.

" Let's get ready. Let's visit them " Avery said and about to go. I pulled her hand.

" No, we are not going " I said a little angrily. Her smile faded off.

" She is your sister. Don't you want to see your nephew ? She just called me. She is so happy. She wants you to visit to see her baby " She said sadly.

Stefen can't you handle ana ? Why did you let her tell Avery ?

" When I say no then no " I said angrily. She removed my hand from her.

" What kind of brother are you ? " She said angrily.

It's dangerous Avery. I can't let you leave this house. I won't leave you a single minute.

I didn't respond to her and about to go.

" MIKE !!!! " Avery yelled angrily.

" IT'S DANGEROUS OUTSIDE " I screamed angrily. She got shocked.

" Dangerous ? "

Shut !!! What did I do.

I walked to her.

" I... Mean.... Ron is kidnapped and... I don't want to take risk. So... " I tried to cover up. Avery came to me and hold my hand.

" It's fine. The kidnapper is arrested. Why are you scared ? " She asked in sad tone.

He is not arrested. If you get to know him then I don't know what happens.

" But... " Before I complete.

" Please... Let's go. I want to see Ana's baby. Didn't you said that you want to spend time and want to be like a normal family. It's the best time " Avery requested.

Avery you are not understanding. It's dangerous. He is Damon. The gangster. He wants you.

I placed my head down. Avery looked at me and turned her back in anger .

" I don't want to talk to you " She said in anger.

If I don't take she will be suspicious.

" fine " In a second Avery turned and hugged me tightly.

" I love you " Avery screamed and kissed my cheek. I smiled.

Avery point of view

The minute we got outside. I got shocked to see there are lots of bodyguards around our car. I hold Ron's hand tightly.

Kidnapper is arrested. Why do we need this much security ?

I seen Mike is talking to one Bodyguard. He walked to me and we inside the car. Mike sat beside me while ron took my right side and Mike took my left side.

" Mike, Do we need this much security ? " I asked looking around. There are 4-5 cars behind our car and 2 in front of our car.

" Ofcourse. I told you I can't take risk " Mike said smiling at me.

" But... " Before I speak.

" Shh.... " Mike placed his finger on my lips. I remained silent.

The minute we reached stefen's house. Bodyguards started to cover us and while Mike hold my hand so tightly whole ron is in his arms.

We got inside while guards stood outside the house.

Stefen got shocked to see us.

" Didn't I told you to bring... " Before stefen complete. Mike gave a look and stefen stopped. Mike placed Ron on floor.

" Ron, Don't go far. " Mike said. Ron nodded and hold my hand.

" Where is Ana ? " I asked stefen.

" She is upstairs " Stefen pointed to upstairs. I am about to go. Mike hold my hand. I looked at him confused.

" Let me come with you " He said.

Come with me. Who is stopping you ? He is behaving strange. Leave it. I want to meet ana.

We walked upstairs. Only to find ana on bed with a small baby. I ran to her.

" Avery, You are finally here " Ana smiled and about to sit. I stopped her.

" Lay down " I said. She did I say. I looked at the small baby. He is so cute.

" Sis, The baby is so small " Ron said and placed his hand on the baby cheek. I smiled and lifted the baby slowly in my hands.

" He looks like you " I said to ana. She smiled.

" Mike, come here. Look, he is so cute " I called him. Mike walked to us. He placed a small kiss on Ana's forehead and came to me. He placed his hand on his cheek and smiled.

" He is cute right ? " I said. Mike nodded and placed his hand on my hair. Before I speak any further suddenly he peed on me. All started to laugh.

" Eww " Ron reacted. While ana, Mike,stefen started to laugh.

" He likes you " Stefen said while laughing.

" Go and wash " Stefen said and lifted him in his arms.

" Avery, pick a pair of clothes. It's in my closet " Ana said. I nodded. I am about to go. Mike hold my hand.

" Let me come with you " Mike said. I nodded.

" Ron, Be with uncle and aunt. Don't go anywhere " Mike warned. He nodded.

" Relax. We are here " Ana said.

We smiled and walked to another room. I am about to walk into the washroom. Mike stopped me.

" What ? " I asked.

" Don't close the door " He said.

What ? Are you serious ?

My eyes widen in shock.

" Mike, I am going to change " I said.

" So what ? We already seen eachother " Mike said. I closed my eyes in irritation. I pushed him and quickly locked the door. I blushed.

" Avery.... " Mike knocked.

" Wait outside " I said.

" Fine. Talk to me. " He said.

What happened to him ? He is behaving strange.

" Mike, I want to shower. Please" I requested.

" Fine " I heard his voice.

I blushed and slowly removed my clothes one by one. I quickly pressed the shower. The warm water hit my body. I started to rub my body with soap slowly. Suddenly I felt a pair of arms around my waist.

Mike..... Where did he find a key to open the door ?

My face has soap. So, I can't open my eyes.

" Mike " I blushed and quickly started to cover myself. Suddenly I left his lips on my shoulder. Water hit my face and soap got removed. The minute I opened my eyes. I looked at the mirror in front of me. My eyes widen in shock.

" Da_mon " That's all got out of my mouth.

Please do like, share and comment.

A new member

Avery point of view

My eyes widen in shock.

Damon ?

I shivered. I turned to him. To get to know is it a bad nightmare.

He is... He is really in front of me.

I am about to scream. He quickly placed his hand on my mouth tightly. That's all tears appeared in my eyes. I started to shiver. I am trying my best to escape.

He is same has he use to be 3 years back.

He wore a black shirt. He has a scar of his forehead which I gave him.

" Avery... " He whispered and looked started to stare all over my body. I closed my eyes in disgust.

I am struggling to let go of his grip from me.

" Wow !!! Your body has become more beautiful " He said staring at my naked body. I am about to scream. He pressed my mouth more tightly and started to on all the taps to not let out my sound.

" You didn't told him the entire truth " He said while smiling at me. My eyes widen in shock.

" I kidnapped your cute little brother. Didn't you husband told you ? " My eyes widen in shock.

Kidnapper ? He kidnapped Ron ? But.. Mike told me that kidnapper is arrested.

He stared at my body again. He looked at the tatoo on my waist.

" Oh !! You have a tatoo of your husbands name " He said while smiling. He slowly moved his hand on my breast. Tears started to flow down my cheek and I nodded as no to him.

" I just want your body. sleep with me" He said in disgust rubbing my breast. I am crying from inside. I can't able to scream. I am about to kick him. He escaped. He looked into my eyes angrily.

" I will get my revenge for what you have done " He said angrily. In a second he bent towards my neck and bite me hardly. I closed my eyes in pain. He pressed his teeth so hardly blood started to come out of my skin.

" I will give you 2 days. Just 2 days. If you don't come to me. I am sure that I will kill your husband and Ron " He said. My eyes widen in shock.

Yes, he will do anything. He will do anything.

" If you tell this to your husband. You know right what will happen ? Rewind the past " He warned.

Past... No... No... I won't let anything happen to ron and Mike.

" If you scream. I will fuck you right now " He said angrily and removed his hand on my mouth. I started to breath hardly. My eyes filled with tears and I am shivering.

" Come with me or see your loved ones died. You know I will do it " He said angrily.

He is taking revenge. He will kill anybody who comes between him.

" You loved that bastard. He was same has me right. Torturing you, Killing you from inside, scaring you " He said angrily looking into my eyes. I quickly covered myself with my hands.

Yes, He was same has you. But... He has a disorder. But.. you... You just want my body.

" Covering won't work " He said angrily and removed my hands. He staring at my xxxxxx and bent down. I closed my eyes tightly.

No, He will do it. He will do it.

Mike, where are you ?

" Avery, are you done ? " Mike screamed. I am about to scream. He quickly closed my mouth again.

" Shh.... One scream. They are dead " He said and pulled out the gun from his pocket. My eye widen in shock.

Gun... This is the same gun... He killed... He killed... My...

" Avery, Why aren't you answering ?" Mike screamed again knocking the door.

Please... Break the door Mike. Save me. Save me.

" I am coming. Say it " He whispered angrily. He placed the gun on my head. My eyes widen in shock.

Please... No...No..

He slowly removed his hand from my mouth. He pressed the gun on my temple.

" I... Am coming " I screamed in tears.

" Are you alright ? " Mike asked. I started crying silently.

No... Please save me Mike.

Damon about to pull trigger.

" YES !!! " I yelled.

" Fine. Come fast, I am waiting " Mike said. I started to cry silently tears are flowing down my cheek.

" Looks like he loves you more " He said. I am just stood there crying.

" 2 days. I am giving you 2 days. " He ordered. He stared at my body again.

" I want to fuck you right now " He said. I just stood there in tears.

" It's fine. I waited for you 2 years. 2 days more. Then, I can fuck you daily " He said disgustingly. He quickly placed a kiss on my lips and parted off.

" I am waiting baby " He said and walked off. I seen he jumped out of the window wearing a wires around his waist.

It's 2nd floor.

I sat on ground and pulled my legs closer to me and started to cry silently.

He is back. He will kill Mike. He will kill Ron.

He is back.

Damon is back.

After a few minutes of crying. I took a quick shower. I dressed up. I wiped my tears and looked myself in mirror. I covered the bite quickly with my air. I made a smile.

Smile... Avery.... Smile.

I smiled and took a deep breath and opened the door. There I seen Mike reading news paper. He looked at me and got up.

" Are you done ? " He asked and smiled.

I can't able to control my tears. I ran to him and hugged him tightly. Mike hugged me.

" What happened ? " Mike asked in worried tone. I pressed my lips tightly to not let out my cry. I nodded as no.

" Look at me " Mike said and broke the hug. There he seen my eyes filled with tears. His eyes widen in shock.

" You are crying ? " Mike asked wiping my tears.

" I.. Missed you " I diverted. Mike looked at me confused. Suddenly he laughed.

" You should've called me. I love couple showers " Mike teased. I just hugged him again.

" Oh !!! Come on. Don't cry like a baby " Mike said tapping my hair.

I won't let anything happen to you. I won't let anything happen to ron. I will protect you. I will sleep with him. To save you. I will sleep with him.

....

We got back to home.

I sat on sofa thinking about the same thing which happened in morning.

What I have to do ? I can't say this to Mike. He is dangerous. He can do anything.

My hands are shaking. He is taking revenge for I have done. He won't let go without taking my body.

I can't let past repeat. I won't let them die just like my parents.

Suddenly I felt I vomiting. I ran to kitchen and started to vomit.

What's happening to me ? Why I am vomiting ?

I quickly washed my mouth. A tear rolled in my eyes.

The only way is to leave Mike. To save them this is the only way.

" Avery " Suddenly I heard Mike voice. I quickly wiped my tears. I turned around and smiled.

" Yes "

" What are you doing here ? " He asked looking at me.

" To drink water " I said. He came to me and took my hand.

" Come " I stopped him.

" Where ? " I asked in confuse.

" I want to show you something " He said while smiling.

What is it ?

" Surprise " He said. I smiled and walked behind him. There I see Ron sat on sofa playing with his toy. He made me sit beside Ron.

" Come " Suddenly Mike called someone. I seen a Bodyguard got inside holding a huge box in his hand.

He placed the box on table and left.

" Pumpkin, open it " Mike said. Ron excitingly started to open the box. Suddenly I got shocked to see a small puppy peeped from the box.

" PUPPY !!!! " Ron yelled and quickly pulled puppy into his arms.

He looks so happy and smiling brightly.

Yesterday he said, he don't like dogs. Why did he brought then ?

I smiled and walked to Mike. I raised my eyebrows to answer the question.

" Do you like it ? " Mike asked and placed his hand around my shoulder.

" You don't like dogs right ? " I asked.

" For pumpkin. I can do anything " He said.

" Thank you Superman " Ron about to come towards for a hug. Mike moved back.

" Place him on ground " Mike said in fear pointing to puppy. I laughed.

" He won't bite superman. He is so cute " Ron said tapping the puppy. Mike quickly hide behind me.

" Save me " Mike requested. I laughed.

" Mike, you are behaving like a small kid " I said while laughing.

" Please... " Mike hold me tightly.

" Fine "

" What name we are going to give him ? " Ron asked. I started to think.

" Sunny " I said.

" Sunny ? " Mike said.

" Hmm, He looks bright " I said while smiling.

" YEHHHH....... Sunny " Ron yelled and started to play with him. Me and Mike smiled at each other looking at Ron.

" Thank you " I said. Mike smiled.

....

I am cleaning bed. Suddenly I felt a pair of arms around my waist. I smiled.

" What ? " I asked and placed my hand on my cheek. Mike placed his head on my shoulder. Mike slowly placed a kiss on my bare shoulder. My stomach filled with butterflies. He slowly moved towards my ear node and started to kiss my ear node.

I am just feeling his touch on my body. Mike moved to my left side of neck and moved my hair aside and about to place a kiss. Suddenly he stopped.

" Bite ? " Mike said. My eyes widen in shock.

He seen the bite made my Damon.

I pulled away from him and covered the bite with my hair. Mike looked at me confused.

" Where did you get that ? " Mike asked looking at me seriously.

What I have to do ?

" It's... It's... "

What I have to say ?

" SUNNY " I yelled. Mike looked at me confused.

" It's... It's... Sunny. I... I... Lifted him. He... He... " I am trying my best to cover. Mike walked to me slowly. I can't able to say further. He just came to me and removed my hairs aside. He looked at my bite closely.

" It's not dog bite " Suddenly his voice turned into anger. He looked at me.

He will get to know. He will know.

He came closer to my face. He took my face in his hands.

" Did... I do it ? " Mike asked. He literally has tears in his eyes.

No....

" Is... My physco is back ? " Mike asked in sad tone. My eyes widen in shock.

He is blaming himself.

" No... It's not you. It's sunny... " Before I complete. Suddenly Mike turned his back to me.

" I... Am hurting you again " Mike said in sad tone. Tears appeared in my eyes seeing him sad. I walked to him. There I seen his eyes turned red with full of tears.

" It's really not you " I said in tears. I am about to touch him.

" Forgive me " Mike said moving back. I got shocked by his behaviour. I walked to him.

" It's really sunny. He bite me. " I said and took his hands. He looked at me in teary eyes.

" I... regret every second for what I did to you in past. I... Don't want anything to repeat again. " Mike said in tears. I pulled him into a tight hug.

" You really didn't do it " I said. He started to cry in my arms.

" Don't leave me even a second " Mike said in his sobs.

Tears started to roll down my cheek.

I have to. To save you. I have to leave you.

I placed a kiss on his lips. Mike pulled me closely. We started to kiss so passionately like there is so tomorrow. Mike lifted me and placed me on bed.

" Let's have a baby " Mike said breathing heavily and placed to kiss. I stopped him.

" We... Already did " I said hesitantly.

" So, what ? " Mike asked and about to kiss on my lips again. I stopped him.

No...... This is the chance to make him hate me.

" I don't like it " I said a little angrily and turned my face. Mike smiled and turned my face to him.

Hate me please. Hate me so much that I can leave you.

" It will not pain " He said while smiling. He pulled my lips and started to kiss. A tear rolled in my eyes.

" No " I said making him stop. Mike moved towards my neck and started to kiss my neck.

" STOP IT !!! " I yelled angrily. Mike looked at me confused. I looked at him angrily. I pushed him from me and got up.

Hate me.

" Are you okay ? " Mike asked coming closer to me. I got up from bed.

" I SAID NO !!! " I screamed angrily. Mike looked at me shockingly. He got up and placed his hand on my cheek.

" Fine. Don't be angry. I should've taken permission from you " Mike said sadly. I can't able to control my tears. I moved back.

" Don't ever touch me " I said angrily pointing my finger to him. Mike got shocked.

" Avery, what happened ? " Mike asked sadly. He almost had tears in his eyes.

Come on!!! Yell at me. Hit me. Do something that hates me.

" It's fine. Come here " Mike said opening his arms. I turned around angrily. I pressed my lips and started to cry silently.

Please hate me.

I felt his hand on my shoulder.

" Is something bothering you ? " Mike asked in worried tone. I didn't turned to him.

Mike point of view

What happened ? Why Avery is behaving strange ?

I can't able to control my tears. I pulled her to me.

" DIDN'T I TOLD YOU TO NOT TOUCH ME !!! " She yelled angrily pushing me. That's all.

My heart stopped for a second. Tears flowing down my cheek.

" Why.... Are you behaving strange ? " I asked in tears.

" Leave me alone " She said and about to go. I pulled her wrist.

" Please.... Tell me " I requested her. Her eyes is full of tears and anger.

" LEAVE ME !!! " She screamed. I pulled her back to me.

" Give me a reason " I asked in tears.

" Just... Leave me " She said in tears. In a second. Avery got unconscious.

" AVERY !!! " I yelled and hold her tightly.

What happened to you ? What's bothering you ? Why are you saying me to leave you ?

Please do like, share and comment.

Hate me

Mike point of view

I seen leah woke up slowly.

" Are you okay ? " I said and about to hold her hand. She moved back.

Why she is behaving like this ?

" I prepared breakfast for you " I said and pulled the tray.

" I don't want it " She said angrily without looking at me.

A pain hit in my heart. What happened Avery ? Why are you avoiding me ?

" You have to eat " I said a little angrily. She turned her face. I placed the tray aside. I took her hand. She is about to remove it. I hold it tightly.

" Why are you punishing me ? Just give me one reason for your behaviour " I said sadly. Suddenly I seen a tear dropped down her cheek. I am about to wipe her tears. She refused. I turned my face tears rolled in my eyes.

I took the tray and about to fed her.

" I DON'T WANT " She screamed and pushed my hand. The spoon landed on floor. My eyes widen in shock tears are in my eyes.

No... I won't do anything which I regret again.

I took a deep breath. I slowly placed my hand on her stomach. She looked at me shockingly.

" Don't you want to feed our baby ? " I said in tears. She looked at me shockingly.

" W_hat did you say ? " She asked shockingly.

" You are pregnant Avery. We are going to have a baby " I said smiling at her. Suddenly I seen a smile on her face.

" Baby " She said. I nodded.

When you got unconscious. Doctor told me this good news. I was so happy that I want to share with you. But... I don't know that reason for your strange behaviour.

" Sunny... Don't run " Suddenly we heard Ron voice. He got inside the room while sunny is running whole room. My eyes widen in shock. I quickly ran to pumpkin.

" Didn't I told you to don't run ? " I warned angrily. Pumpkin Suddenly can't able to breath.

" Ron " Avery got up from bed and ran to us. She hold Ron hands.

" Pumpkin, where is your inhaler ? " I asked. He just started to breath hardly. I suddenly remembered that I have a spare inhaler. I quickly ran to my cupboard and pulled out a inhaler. I ran to Pumpkin and sprayed it into his mouth.

Avery point of view

He made Ron live like a half dead person.

He didn't spare a small kid. He will do anything to kill Mike.

" Is it fine ? " Suddenly Mike asked to ron. Ron nodded.

" Didn't I told you to keep the inhaler with you ? " I said angrily. Ron started to cry.

" Avery, He is kid. We have to let him understand, not scare him " Mike said and quickly hugged Ron.

You guys have to hate me.

There is only 1 day left. I have to make you guys hate me then I can leave forever happily.

Being Mike I can rest assured. He can take good take of Ron.

" This stupid dog. I am going to chase him out " I said angrily and quickly picked up the sunny.

" Sis, No... I want sunny " Ron started to cry and clenched my shirt. Mike looked at me shockingly.

" Give sunny to him " Mike said angrily.

" He made... " Before I speak. Mike quickly pulled the sunny from me and handed it to ron.

He hate dogs right ?

" Don't cry " Mike said wiping Ron's tears. A pain hit in my heart. When I seen Ron crying badly. This the only way to make you hate me.

Ron stopped crying. Mike lifted Ron in his arms while he took my hand. He made me sit on bed and Mike got seated.

" Say sorry to sis " Mike said. Ron pouted angrily.

" Sis is worried about you. Didn't she already warned to not run? " Mike said. Ron nodded.

" I am sorry, sis " Ron said and quickly placed sunny on floor and about to hug me. I turned face. Ron stopped.

" Avery ? " Mike hold my hand. The minute I turned Ron hugged me so tightly. A tear rolled down my cheek. I hugged him so tightly.

I won't let anything happen to you. I will sacrifice myself for you guys.

I broke the hug and smiled at Ron.

" Feeling better " Mike whispered. My eyes widen.

I am making him hate me. He still care about me.

I nodded.

" Pumpkin, Go play " Mike said and placed him on ground.

" Slowly " I warned. Ron nodded and walked out with sunny. I smiled. Suddenly I heard Mike started to stare at me.

" What ? " I asked a little angrily. Mike smiled.

" You look cute, when you're angry " Mike said. I blushed. Mike pulled me closer to him.

" Thank you " He said.

" Why ? "

" Giving me a beautiful family " He said placing his hand on my stomach.

" So, you didn't used any thing that day " I asked. Mike raised his eyebrows.

" Anything ? "

" I... Mean... I... Mean... " I am trying to say.

" You mean condoms ? " Mike asked. My eyes widen in shock.

Yes, But... How can he say so easily ?

" I Never wanted to use them " Mike said. Mike pulled me more closer. He removed my hair locks behind my ear.

" Will you tell me the reason behind your anger ? " Mike asked calmly. I quickly pulled away from me and got up. Mike looked at me shockingly.

" I want to use washroom " I ignored him and about to go. Mike pulled my wrist.

" We have to talk " Mike said. I removed his hand and walked into the washroom.

The minute I locked the door. I leaned on door and started to cry silently.

I... Am sorry.

Damon is a dangerous man. He will do anything.

He killed my parents. He is taking revenge.

He will kill you guys too. I can't loose a family again.

I walked to a mirror. I placed my hand on stomach.

I... Am pregnant. What happens when Damon know this ?

He is going to kill my baby. Tears started to flow down my cheek. I sat there and started crying badly.

....

The minute I came out I didn't seen Mike anywhere. Suddenly my phone buzzed.

Unknown number.

I picked up the call.

" Babe " The voice made me shiver. My eyes widen in shock. My hands started to shake.

" I prepared so much for you babe. You are coming tomorrow. I will be waiting for you at Dolphin street on my car "

My eyes widen in shock. He.. he.. gave me 2 days. 2 days is not yet completed.

" You.... You gave me 2 days. It's... Not completed yet " I said in fear. I heard a laugh on other side.

" The day I said to you counts babe. I am eager to eat your body " He said disgustingly.

Tears rolled down my cheek.

I have only today to spend the last days with them.

" Do whatever. But... At 10:00pm, I want you in my car " He warned.

" Did you know there is a secret Bodyguard in your group who helps me. The minute you do something stupid he will not think a second to kill them " He said angrily. My eyes widen in shock.

" Waiting for you babe " He placed a kiss on phone. I quickly hung up the call.

I have to leave tomorrow. I have to.

" Avery, you didn't eat morning. I prepared... " Suddenly I heard Mike voice. I wiped my tears and turned to him. He placed the tray on table and quickly walked to me. He took my face in his hands.

" You look pale " Mike said in worried tone. I just kept on staring at him.

This is the last day to see you.

" Avery ? " I blinked my eyes. I looked at his worried face.

" Yes "

" You are hungry. Let's eat " Mike said smiling at me.

Why don't you hate me ?

" I...am not hungry " I said and about to leave Mike pulled my hand.

" Why are you being like this ? " Mike asked in sad tone. I seen tears in his eyes.

" I am not hungry " I said angrily and removed his hand. Mike looked at me sadly.

" You have to eat " Mike said a little angrily. I am about to leave.

" Eat for the baby " Mike said. I controlled my tears. I turned around. There I seen tears rolled down his cheek. He quickly wiped them. He walked to tray and got seated.

" Come " Mike said tapping on bed. I stood there still. I seen Mike controlling his anger as much as possible.

Yell at me Mike. Slap at me.

Be angry at me.

" Fine. Don't eat " Mike said angrily. In a second he walked out of the room.

Tears rolled down my cheek. I sat on ground and started crying.

Suddenly in a second my arm being pulled up and without even a second a kiss is being placed on my lips.

I opened my eyes only to see Mike kissing me. I seen tears rolling down his cheek.

He started moving the lips slowly. He pulled my waist tightly. He stopped and closed his eyes and attached his forehead with my forehead. We are so close that our nose are touching.

" I... Don't want to show my tears. But... When you be like this. I can't stop my tears. I don't the reason behind your behaviour. You not even got excited when I said you are pregnant. Just give me one reason. One reason. Please " Mike requested in tears. I seen his eyes are closed tears are flowing down his cheek. I lifted my hand to wipe his tears and stopped. I stood still in tears.

" Don't want to answer. Fine, be angry at me. But... Please eat " Mike said sadly.

I can't see him like this.

" I will eat " I said. He quickly opened his eyes and placed a kiss on my lips.

" Thank you " Mike said. I seen a smile on his face.

....

" Here " Mike said giving me the medicines. I took them. Mike sat beside me. He pulled the magazine and started to read.

Don't he leave home. How can I plan to escape ?

I am about to get up. Mike took my hand.

" Where are you going ? " Mike asked quickly.

" I... Want to see Ron " I lied.

" I will come too " Mike said and about to get up.

" I can go, you read magazine " I said and about to go. Mike hold my hand tightly.

" I am coming " Mike said and got up.

Why he is being stuck to me ?.

Won't he have any work.

I can't make a fight again. I made him cry already.

We walked to Ron's room only to find him playing with sunny.

I am leaving tommorow Ron. Today is the only day I can spend time with you.

I have to make you forget about me. I have to make you hate me.

I walked to ron angrily and pulled sunny from his hand and placed him on ground.

" Don't you have school today ? Playing with dog " I yelled angrily. Mike looked at me shockingly. While ron started to cry. Mike walked to ron and lifted him in his arms.

" Stop the act !!! You are going to turn six. Stop behaving like a child " I yelled angrily controlling my tears.

" Avery " Mike made me stop. He started to tap Ron's back.

" I hate you " Ron said in sobs.

Tears rolled in my eyes.

He hates me.

Good. Forget about me Ron. From now on Mike is everything to you.

" Come here " I angrily pulled Ron from Mike's arms.

" Avery, listen to me " Before Mike speak. I pulled him. I lifted my hand to hit him.

" AVERY !!!! " Mike yelled angrily.

Please hate me. Hate me.

" What ? He is my brother. I have right to do what I want " I said angrily Mike looked at me shockingly. While ron kept on crying.

" Uncle " Ron started to move into Mike's arms. Mike quickly pulled Ron into his arms.

Tears rolled in my eyes. I can't able to control my tears. I walked out of the room.

I started to cry placing my hand on my mouth.

I am sorry... I am sorry Ron. I never raised my hand on you.

After a few minutes. I heard foot steps.

It must be Mike. I quickly wiped my tears.

" Come with me " Mike said and in a second he pulled my hand.

" Where are you taking me ? Leave my hand " I said removing his hand. He pulled me into our bedroom. He released my hand and walked to his closet and started to pull out all his clothes.

What is he doing ?

He pulled out his dairy.

Dairy ?

He walked to me and threw the dairy on bed. He looks angry. He walked to me and pulled my shoulders.

He looks angry. He hates me too.

" Do you know, what today is ? " Mike asked a little angrily.

Today ? Is it special ?

I stood still not answering his question.

" You said, you read my dairy right ? Then, don't you know what today is ? " Mike asked in sad tone.

What today is ?

Mike pulled the dairy from bed and opened the back page of the dairy. He gave it to me.

I looked into it.

" May 5 - My birthday "

My eyes widen in shock.

Today is his birthday. It's important day and I made him cry. I am not qualified to be his wife.

He pulled the dairy and threw it on bed.

He pulled my face in his hands. Tears rolled in my eyes.

" I... Am waiting since morning that you gone wish me. But... Your strange behaviour I don't get it " Mike said in sad tone. Small tears are in his eyes.

I gone through your dairy. But... I didn't seen your birthday date in it.

" Ever since we came from stefen's home. You started to being strange, what is bothering you ? " Mike asked in tears. I stood still not even given him a single answer.

" Your behaviour on Ron. What that small child did to you ? If you're angry at me. Be angry at me. But... Don't yell at Ron. I hardly made him sleep. He is hating you. You don't want him to hate you right ? " Mike asked in sad tone.

" I... Want him to hate me " I said angrily looking into his eyes. Mike eyes widen in shock. He furrow his eye brows.

" Hate you ? Why ? " Mike asked sadly. Tears dropped down my cheek.

" I.. can't able to handle this family. I want a break " I said angrily.

" Break ? Are you stressed ? How about we go on a trip for few days ? " Mike asked and placed a small smile. I removed his hands from my face.

Don't you hate me Mike ? You still worried about me.

I moved back and placed my hand on stomach.

Mike stared at my hand.

" You are a liar. You didn't used any protection that day and because of you, I am pregnant right now " I yelled angrily in tears. Mike got shocked. He got numb and moved back a step. A tear dropped down his cheek.

" W_hat did you say ? " Mike asked in tears.

" I..... " Before I say.

" Do.... you even know what you're saying ? " Mike asked in tears.

I... Am sorry. I... Am sorry.

I am about to leave. Mike pulled my wrist. He pulled me closer to my chest.

" WHAT ? " I yelled. I looked at his red and teary eyes.

I never seen him like this. He looks life less.

" It's... My birthday " Mike said in tears. I controlled my tears. I took a deep breath.

" So, what ? Do I dance in front of you naked ? Or Do you want me to sleep with you ? " I chuckled.

That's all. A hard slap got hit on my face. I placed my hand on cheek.

While Mike turned his back and placed his hand on his forehead and his hands are shaking.

Tears continuously flowing down my cheek.

Thank you for hating me Mike.

....

It's 8:00pm.

We didn't spoke about the incident happened last night.

Mike is not in home. Ron, Don't want to see me.

I lost everyone. I lost family.

I stood in balcony. I started to recall the incident happened in his balcony.

This Is the same place where I first got feelings for him. I felt feelings when he kissed me here.

I started to recall all the incidents happened.

How can I escape from this house ? There are bodyguards around the house.

Suddenly I heard a voice inside the kitchen. I walked towards the kitchen only to find Mike about to place his hand on stove. My eyes widen in shock. I ran to him and pulled his hand. He got Burn a little on his palm.

" What are you doing ? " I said in worried tone and started to blow on his wound. A tear rolled in my eyes.

" Come here " I took his wrist and took him to living room and made him sit on sofa. I ran and searched for first aid. I found it. I ran to Mike.

" Give me your hand " I said opening the box and pulled out a spirit and cotton. He sat still. I looked Into his eyes.

His eyes are red with full of tears and pain. I stopped staring at him and took his hand.

I slowly placed the cotton on his wound. I looked at him to look it's paining. He sat still in tears.

I blow slowly on his wound and bandage it. I am about to get up.

Mike hold my hand.

" I... Am sorry " Mike said placing his head down.

It's my fault. I made your birthday a disaster.

I sat beside him. Mike looked at me in guilty and tears are in his eyes.

He slowly placed his hand on my stomach.

" Baby, Tell your mom to forgive me. Daddy loves mom. He can't live without her " Mike said in tears. A tear rolled down my cheek.

I can't see him like this. I pulled him into a tight hug. Mike started to sob in my arms. He hugged me tightly and started to cry.

" I.. don't want my birthday to be like this. It's my first birthday with you. I planned everything to make it special. But.. " Mike said in tears.

What kind of stupid wife I am.

" Look at me " I said and broke my hug. Mike looked at me with those tears eyes. I wiped his tears.

" Forget about me " I said in tears. He furrowed his eyebrows and looked at me confused. I can't able to control my tears and about to leave.

" Wait " Mike said shockingly. He wiped his tears. He slowly walked to me and hold my face in his hands and kissed my lips.

He kissed me softly.

After a long kiss. Mike looked at me.

" Don't ever say that " A tear dropped down my cheek.

It's our last kiss Mike.

Please do like ,share and comment.

Letter

Mike point of view

I stretched my arms. I placed my hand beside me. It's felt empty. I opened my eyes quickly.

I didn't seen Aver any where. I got off the bed. I searched around the room. I didn't seen her.

Panic started in me. Where did she go ?

May be in kitchen. I ran to kitchen. I didn't seen her. Suddenly I seen a cake is placed on dinning table.

Cake ? It must be Avery.

This girl really made me worry.

I walked to table. A smile appeared on my face. I found a small letter on the table. I picked up. I unfold the paper.

" Happy Birthday !!!!!

Wish you a many more happy returns of the day Mike.

I don't know what flavor do you like. So, I prepared chocolate cake hope you like it.

I know it's a late wishes. I hope my wishes brings you a lots of happiness. "

Where did she go ? Writing a letter. Where is she hiding ?

I looked around and continued with the letter.

" I am sorry for hurting you. But.... I love you Mike. I love you so much. I know that the kidnapper is not found yet. His name is Damon. "

My eyes widen in shock. She knows the truth.

" Damon is dangerous Mike. He is gangster. He will go anything to kill you or Ron. He... He... Killed my parents Mike. "

Past of Avery.

" Mom, I am leaving " I said and pulled my purse and about to leave.

" You didn't had breakfast " mom yelled.

" I will eat in canteen mom. I am gone be late " I am about to leave. Dad stopped me.

" Dad "

" Health comes first " Dad warned. I smiled.

" Fine " I said and got seated on dinning table while mom started to place the dishes. There my cute little brother crawling in ground playing with toys.

" Ron, My cuteee... " I said and lifted him in my arms.

" Avery, Give Ron to dad. Have breakfast first " Mom said. I placed a kiss on Ron's cheek and handed him to dad and I am about to eat. Suddenly we heard calling bell. I am about to get up.

" You eat. I am going to see " Mom said and walked to door. Suddenly he heard a huge sound. Dad and me ran to living room. Only to see mom found dead on floor.

" MOM !!! " I cried and ran to her. I seen Damon walked into the room. He has 2-3 bodyguards behind him. He is holding gun in his hand.

" You... " Dad about to pull his collar. He pushed dad. Dad fell on ground. While I seen Ron crying badly.

" Dad " i walked to dad. And started to cry.

" Didn't I told you to come to my bedroom last night ? " Damon screamed angrily. I started to shiver.

" What... He is saying ? " Dad asked in tears holding Ron tightly.

" Please... Leave us " I said begging in front of him.

" Leave. I won't leave until I have your body completely " Damon screamed. He pulled me up.

" Looks like you have bedroom. Let's do it here " Damon about to pull me to bed room. Dad hold his leg tightly.

" Leave my daughter " Dad screamed. He kicked dad.

" No, I will... Sleep with you. Don't do anything to them " I said in tears. Dad about to stop. Bodyguards stopped him. He dragged me into the bedroom and locked the door.

" The first time I seen you. I am damn waiting to sleep with you. Your body, Your lips, your eyes, everything I want it. I warned you last night. If you don't sleep with me. I am going to kill your family. Look your mom died. I will kill your father too " He said walking towards me.

" No.... Do whatever you want with me. But.... Please don't kill my family " I begged helplessly. He smiled and in a second he removed his shirt. He walked to me and ripped my shirt. He threw me on bed. He got on me. He pulled my bra. He started to kiss my every part.

Why ? Why it's Happening to me ?

" Ah... You smell so beautiful " He said licking my breasts. Tears started to flow down my cheek. He is about to remove my pants. I am struggling hard to get out of his grip.

" STAY STILL " He yelled. He got out of control. He quickly walked out and in a second I heard a gun shot sound.

I got numb. I can only hear Ron's crying.

He killed father.

He walked inside.

" Satisfy me. Nor, next is your little brother " He said and climbed on bed.

I will kill you Damon. You never gone get my body. He started to kiss my neck. I found a vase beside bed. I pulled it and quickly hit on his head.

" AH.... " He yelled. .

" Master, are you okay ? " Bodyguard yelled from outside.

" Ah... Damon slowly " I acted.

" Looks like having fun. let's wait outside " I heard them. He is about to speak. I hardly hit on his face.

" You....bitch " He said in pain.

" You won't get my body " He said angrily.

" I... Will.... Come back to you. I will have your body. I... Will get revenge " He said holding his bleeding head. I pushed him. He got unconscious.

I ran out of the room. I seen Ron crying badly. I quickly picked him up. I lastly looked at dad and mom.

I... Am sorry. I am horrible child for not burriying you guys. But... Ron is only left. I can't let him die.

I hold there bodies and started to cry.

" BITCH !!! " Suddenly Damon yelled. My eyes widen.

" Sir yelled " Bodyguards shouted. I quickly escaped from there.

....

" I... Am sorry for not saying the whole truth. He will do anything to get me Mike. Please don't search for me. Always remember that I love you. I will always love only you.

I didn't seen porns Mike. I experienced it in real life.

Please look after Ron. He is my life. Say him that I love him. I will always love him. Please... Don't let him hate me.

Give my love to stefen and Ana. I got a wonderful family.

I was happy when you said I am pregnant. I promise you I won't let anything happen to our child.

Your love is in my womb. I won't let it hurt.

I... Am sorry.

Love you   Avery. "

After reading. My legs felt numb. I got seated on ground. Tears continuously flowing down my cheek.

What have you done stupid. You should've told me all this. We would've handled it together.

Why did you leave me ? Why ? Why ?

Where am I going to find you now ?

It's my fault. I should've understood more.

I had done same with you. I too tortured you.

I started to hit myself hardly.

The PYSCO in me made you Suffered too.

I am same has Damon too. The difference is that I married you. He didn't. I too killed you from inside.

I started to cry and cry.

" Mike " I heard a voice. There I seen stefen and ana walked to me.

" Avery... Left me stefen. She left me Ana " i cried holding the paper. They looked at me sadly and took the paper from my hand. They started to read.

" Get up. Let's find Avery " Stefen said making me get up. I nodded as no.

" There..... is nothing left to find " I said in tears.

" You are stupid Mike. She must be around here. Let's find her. He can't get Avery " Ana said angrily. My eyes widen.

Yes, She must be here. She can't escape when they are lots of bodyguards.

I ran out. I quickly ran outside.

" Did you seen Avery ? " I asked bodyguards at entrance.

" Isn't mam at home ? " he answered.

How did you escaped avery ?

" Is any bodyguard is missing ? " I asked. He looked at all. He started to think.

" Sir, A bodyguard is missing " A man ran to me. My eyes widen in shock.

He is Damon's man. How did I made such a huge mistake ?

" SEARCH AROUND !!! " I yelled. They got dispersed.

....

After 9 hours.

" Did you find them ? " Stefen asked quickly to bodyguards and inspector. They nodded as no.

I got numb and got seated on chair.

I lost Avery. I lost her.

" Leave... Me alone " I said lifeless.

" Mike " Stefen about to say.

" LEAVE ME ALONE " I yelled in tears. All about to walk outside.

" Ana " I called her. She turned to me sadly in tears.

" Yes " She walked to me and hold my hand.

" Please.... Handle Ron " I requested. She nodded in tears. I turned my back. They walked outside.

I started to cry and cry.

I lost you. I lost you Avery.

I am idiot that I can't able to get you.

Do like, share, comment.

So, Guess what's going to be next ?

What it's going to be? Do they going to meet ?

Any ideas !!!

How you guys want me to end this story ?

Please don't be a silent readers. Please comment me. Being a writer. I feel disappointed.

I know this chapter is too short. I promise that the next chapter gone be blast.

Next chapter gone be interesting. Stay tuned to it.

Avery

Mike point of view

It's been 5 months. I didn't find Avery. I searched her every where.

I can't able to find her.

I stood in front of large window. It's so cold outside. I placed my hands into my pockets.

" Uncle " I heard pumpkin voice. I turned around.

He grown up. My little pumpkin has grown a lot. If Avery would be here. She would be more happy.

I heard brack sound from behind.

There sunny. He grown a lot too.

" Pumpkin " I smiled and kneeled down and hugged him tightly.

" Uncle, look sunny destroyed my colours " Pumpkin complained pointing to sunny There I seen sunny sat there like he didn't so anything. He is totally covered with colour all over his body. I smiled.

" Come here " I said. Soon sunny walked to me waving his tail. I tapped his head.

" Sunny, you are being mischievous day by day " I warned. He sadly placed his head down.

" Now say sorry to ron " I said. He slowly walked to ron and placed his paw on Ron's hand. Ron pulled him into a tight hug.

" Uncle, When sister going to come ? " Suddenly his question made me numb.

I told them that Avery went aboard to do some business and will be back soon. Ever since Avery left I tried so hard to make him sleep daily and made him eat.

But... The days going further. How am I going to handle him ?

" Uncle ? " I came out of my thoughts. I placed my hand on his face.

" Soon "

Ron placed his head down sadly.

" You are saying this from past 5 months. You not even giving her a call. " Ron said sadly. I controlled my tears.

" She is busy. I just called her, She said she is going to bring you lots of toys when she is back " I lied.

" Really ? " Ron got excited. I nodded. He jumped into my arms. A tear rolled in my eyes.

Where are you Avery ?

Suddenly my phone buzzed. I broke the hug and got up. While ron went out with sunny.

Stefen.

I picked up the call.

" Yes " I said.

" When are you leaving ? " He asked.

" Today at 7:00pm " I said.

I am going to switzerland for a business. I got involved in my work to make me divert myself.

I started working day and night.

" You just came yesterday. You are going to different places for business all the weeks without a break. Didn't I told you to take a break ? You gone neglect your health " Stefen said angrily. I sighed.

" Take care of Ron. I will... " Before I continue.

" How many days you are going this time ? 1 day, 5 days, 15 days or.... " Before he continue. A tear rolled in my eyes.

" Ever since Avery left you. You hardly live in that house. Business trips had became your daily routine. When are you going to stop this ? " Stefen yelled.

" Stefen " I called.

" We are worried about you. You didn't visit to see your nephew. You Don't let anyone meet you. Are you planning to become a monster again ? " Stefen said sadly.

" I am going to send Ron. He... " Before I continue.

" Don't let him run. Don't let him out of our sight. Always let him keep the inhaler with him. I know. I know all this, you're saying this from past 5 months " Stefen said angrily.

" Let's have lunch before you leave " Stefen sighed.

" I have to pack my luggage " I said.

" But... " Before he continue. I hung up the call. A tear rolled down my cheek.

....

I reached switzerland. I got out of the flight. Bodyguards, My staff, Started to walk behind me.

" Sir, you have a metting with John Salvatore at 10:00am. Then.. " before my assistant continue. I showed my hand to stop. He stopped. We started to walk and quickly we reached the car. I got inside the car. I started to do my work in laptop. The car stopped at signal.

I peeped out of the window. When I seen a little boy selling dumplings on the street in a small stall.

I love Dumplings.

Avery words remained me.

I am about to get out.

" Sir " My assistant stopped me.

" Park the car. I am gone buy some dumplings " I said looking the shop.

" Sir, I will order you the best dumplings. It's street... " Before he continue. I gave him a angry look. He nodded. I got out of my car. I crossed the road.

Every women started to stare at me. I ignored them and walked to the shop.

" How much ? " I asked.

" 10 Franc " He said smiling at me. I nodded and pulled out my purse from the pocket.

The minute I opened it. I have my credit cards, notes. I don't have coins.

I pulled out the note and gave it to him.

" Sir, I don't have change " He said sadly.

" It's fine. Keep it " I said and took the Dumplings from him. He smiled.

I looked for my car. There my assistant waved his hand. I walked to the direction and got seated in car.

I pulled out the dumplings from cover. I took a bite of it.

Delicious. If Avery would be here. I would've brought her lots of dumplings.

we reached motel. I got off the car while my assistant ran to reception desk and fill the details. I got on sofa. He ran to me.

" sir, room 1026 " He said and gave me the keys. I took them.

" sir, meeting is at 10:00 am " He said.

" I will be there " i said and walked towards the elevator.

....

The minute I reached the room. I directly walked to washroom to take a warm shower.

The warm water hit on my body. A tear rolled down my cheek. I brushed the hair back with my hand.

How are you avery ? How is our baby ?

I came out of the washroom. I wrapped myself with bath rob.

" Lady, Are you okay ? " Suddenly i heard a scream from outside.

who it is ?

I opened my door. I can't see clearly what's going on there. It's crowded. I stopped a man who is running towards the incident.

" what happened ?" I asked.

" A lady got unconscious " He said. I tried to peep but i can't see anything.

I have work to do. I ignored the incident and walked inside and locked the door.

I pulled out my laptop and about to work. Avery picture is on my wall paper. I placed my hand on screen.

I miss you avery.

Tears dropped down my cheek. I quickly wiped them off. I continued with my work.

After working for 2 hours. I heard a knock on the door. I got up and moved the door.

" Sir, It's time for meeting " He said. I nodded. I am so tired.

" Give me 5 minutes " I said.

" Sir, You worked again. It's was your rest time. You still worked. It's important meeting you have to..." Before he complete.

" I will be there " I said and closed the door. I am dizzy. I should've taken some rest.

I am going to be late.

I dressed up and walked downstairs.

" Sir, They are waiting in the restaurant " Assistant said showing me the direction. I walked.

I am busy that I arranged the meeting in resturant of this hotel. I don't want to waste time.

The minute I walked all stood up. I got seated.

" Please be seated " I said. All got seated. We started to discuss about out business. I hold the papers in my hands and hearing there views. Suddenly my eyes rolled to my left.

There I seen a women's back. She is mopping the floor. She is so far. I can't see clearly. I am little dizzy that I can't able to focus on her.

She looks familiar.

" Mike Wilson " I came out of my thoughts.

" Yes, I am listening " I said and concentrated on business.

" BITCH !!! " Suddenly we heard someone yelling. We all turned to the direction.

The women i seen earlier is being scolded by a lady.

I can't able to see clearly what's happening.

" Jackson " I whispered to my Assistant.

" Yes sir " He moved closer to me.

" What happening there ? " I asked.

" Looks like someone bullying the pregnant lady " He said.

Pregnant lady ?

I looked into the direction. In a blink of eye. I seen Avery.

Avery ?

My eyes widen in shock. I can't see clearly. My damn eyes. I am dizzy.

I pulled the glass of water on the table and quickly sprinkled on my face and wiped my face. I looked at that direction. I didn't seen anyone there.

" Where are those people ? " I asked quickly to Jackson.

" They... Left sir "Jackson said shockingly by my behavior. I got up quickly.

" Meeting is dismissed " I said.

" WHAT ? " All yelled at once in confuse. I ignored them and ran towards that direction.

I didn't seen them.

She looks just like Avery. Jackson said pregnant women. She must be Avery.

" Sir, meeting... " Jackson continue.

" Find the pregnant women who was just here " I said quickly looking around.

" Sir... "

" GO !!! " I yelled angrily. He nodded and ran.

After a few minutes I seen jackson came with a Person with him.

" Sir, He is manager here " I walked to him.

" Yes sir, Is my staff made you unhappy ? Let me get you... " Before he continue.

" I just seen a pregnant women mopping here. I want to see her " I said angrily. He got scared.

" Pregnant women ? " He asked in confuse.

" Yes " Jackson said quickly. I am eagerly waiting for his answer.

" Let me call all my staff " He said. After a minutes I seen all people stood on line.

But... I didn't seen any pregnant women here.

" Are you sure you seen pregnant women ? " I asked to Jackson.

" Yes sir. Why would I lie to you ? " He said.

" Where is the pregnant women ? " Jackson asked angrily. Manager panicked.

" WHERE ALL STAFF ? " Manger yelled angrily at staff. They got scared.

" Sir... You mean... Lisa ? " Suddenly a women spoke in fear. My eyes widen.

Lisa ?

" Lisa ? Are you speaking about the pregnant women ? " I asked quickly.

She looked at me.

" Yes sir. She is the only pregnant women who works here " She said.

" Then, where is she ? " I asked a little angrily.

" S_ir.... Her shift is done. She went to home " She said in fear.

" Give me her address " I said angrily.

" But... "

" Do has the customer wants. Don't you know who he is ? He is famous business man " Manger yelled at her. She quickly nodded and pulled out the paper from her pocket and started to write.

I took the paper. I looked into the address.

" Are you ok sir ? Is anything bothering you ? " Manager asked making a smile on his face. I ignored him and walked out of the hotel. I quickly took my car.

Whatever she may be. I have to make sure it is Avery or not. Because I seen her just now. My eyes can't lie.

I raised the speed. After a few hours. I reached the place.

This place is so far.

The minute I looked at the building my eyes widen in shock.

The building looks old and rusted and dirty all over.

I looked at the address.

5th floor.

How can a pregnant lady lives on 5th floor ?

Elevator. I am about to take elevator. I seen " on service "

What kind of stupid building ? Can't able to provide the services for people ?

I took the stairs. I started to run to upstairs.

Huff... Huff.....

I can't able to climb. How can a pregnant women climb this many stairs ?

Finally I reached the floor. I looked into the address.

Room : 101

I searched. Finally I found it. I took a deep breath.

Please.... Let it be Avery. I want to ask her so many questions.

I slowly pressed the calling bell.

After a few seconds. The door started to open slowly. My heart started to beat fastly.

" Yes " I raised my head. My eyes widen in shock to see what's in front of me.

" Avery " That's all came out of my mouth.

So, that's the end of the chapter. Please do like,share and comment.

Lisa

Mike point of view

My eyes widen in shock to see Avery in front of me. I can't describe how she is right now. She wore most a torn dress. Her face looks dull and pale. I didn't seen a smile on her face . I seen a huge bump. I ran to her and hugged her tightly.

" Do you know how many months I have been searching for you ? " I said. Tears rolled in my eyes. Suddenly Avery pushed me hardly.

" Excuse me ? " She said angrily. I looked her in confused.

" Avery ? "

" Lisa, who is it ? " Suddenly I heard a voice from behind. I seen a man came out. He wore the apron. My eyes widen in shock.

Damon !!!! Bastard.

" BASTARD !!! " I yelled and pulled his collar angrily.

" Leave him " Avery started to stop me.

" He made our life hell. I will kill him today " I shouted angrily and about to punch him.

" LEAVE MY HUSBAND " Avery yelled angrily.

Husband ?

My eyes widen in shock. I loosen the grip from his collar.

" John, are you okay ? " She hold that man tightly. I seen her worried face.

Avery won't remember me ? Did she lost her memory ? No, I can't let him live with this bastard.

" Avery, I am your husband. Mike Wilson " I said and about to touch her. She shook my hand.

" Who are you ? Why are you beating my husband ? " She said angrily looking worried at that man.

Damon, what have you done to Avery ? If she is not Avery than the pregnancy. She is pregnant. Avery is pregnant too. By now she will be 5 months pregnant too.

" Lisa, Doctor told you to rest. Get up. Don't cry " He said holding her and placed his hand on her stomach. He wiped her tears.

" Sorry sir. You must've got into wrong room. She is my wife. " He said calmly.

Look at his acting.

" Avery, I know he is black mailing you. Don't worry, I will handle it. Let's leave " I am about to hold her hand. She pushed me.

" What are you doing ? I am not your wife. I am Lisa. I am not Avery who you are talking about " She said angrily.

Acting with him Avery. A tear rolled in my eyes.

" Avery, I don't know what this bastard done to you. But... " Before I speak. Suddenly Avery gave a hard slap on my face. I hold my cheek and my eyes widen in shock.

" HOW DARE YOU CALL MY HUSBAND BASTARD ? " She shouted angrily.

" Lisa, Let's listen to him. He must be searching for his wife "

Bastard....

I am about to punch him.

" STOP IT !!! " Avery yelled angrily.

" What do you want ? Do you have any proof that I am your wife ? " Avery asked.

Proof ? You are asking proof Avery ?

I quickly pulled out my wallet. It's the photo of me and Avery on out wedding day.

I showed to Avery. Her eyes widen in shock.

" She looks exactly like me. Look John " she said showing the picture to him.

Did you lost your memory Avery ?

" Yes " He said shockingly.

This bastard is acting.

I pulled his collar angrily again.

" Did she lost her memory ? Tell her. Tell her that I am her husband. Tell her that you kidnapped her " I said angrily.

" Leave him " Avery said making me stop. I pulled his collar more tightly. He looked at me sadly.

" Sir... " He can't able to breath.

" J_ohn.... " Suddenly we heard Avery hold her stomach tightly. My eyes widen in shock. I loosen my grip.

" Lisa, Is it paining ? I told you to rest " He said holding her. He looks worried. She lifted her in his arms quickly and walked inside.

Avery...

I quickly got inside. The minute I got inside. I shock to see the house is full of they pictures. I seen a wedding picture too.

What's happening here ? Is it really not Avery ?

" Lisa, Breath " Suddenly I heard a sounds from inside. The minute I got inside the bedroom. I seen her on bed while he holding her hand tightly.

Tears rolled down my cheek. She is really not Avery. He is not Damon. If he is Damon he wouldn't be like this.

" Are you okay ? " He asked. She nodded. Suddenly she looked at me and turned her head. A pain hit in my heart.

John walked to me.

" Sir, we are middle class family. Please don't harm us. My wife is pregnant and weak. We got shocked to know that your wife look exactly like my wife. I hope you find your wife soon. Please leave sir " He requested sadly. A tear rolled down my cheek.

You are not Avery.

I finally gave a look at her. While she didn't even looked at me.

" I... Am sorry to disturb you guys. I.. am sorry " I looked at her finally and without turning back. I walked out.

The minute I walked out. I can't able to control my tears. I started to cry silently.

Where are you Avery ?

....

I kept on crying thinking about Avery. It's been 3 days. I am done with my business but I don't want to leave. I just want to see her once.

I just want to see her who resembles Avery. Just once.

" Room service " Suddenly I heard a voice. I ignored it. Tears started to flow down my cheek.

I hold my head.

" Sir... " I heard her voice stopped.

" I don't want. You can leave " I said placing my head down.

" You... "

I raised my head only to see her again. My eyes widen in shock. I got up and. About to got to her. She is about to leave.

" I won't harm you " I said sadly. She stopped.

" I... Misunderstood you has my wife. She... Is pregnant too so... " I about to finish.

" It's fine sir " She is about to leave.

" Just a minute " I said. She stopped. I walked and stood in front of her.

She looks exactly like Avery. Why I do feel strange ?

I looked at her dump.

" I... Have to leave sir " She said playing her head down.

" I.. just want to give tip to you " I said and pulled my wallet from my pocket and pulled 10 notes and handed to her.

" It's... It's... Huge " She said. I smiled.

" It's fine. Seeing you I thought of my wife. Take it has a bonus " I said. She took it. She didn't even once looked at me.

" How months pregnant you are ? " I asked looking at her bump. She felt awkward.

" Don't be scared. I am just asking because you are pregnant. You should rest. I will talk to manger here they will give you off without debit salary " I said looking at her. She still placed her head down.

" It's... It's... Fine sir. If we don't work daily we can't... Affort food " She said. I looked at her sadly.

" Wait here " I said and quickly walked to my bed and pulled out the cover. I just ordered dumplings. Avery loved dumplings hope she will like it too.

I walked to her.

" Here " I said giving her. She looked at the cover confusingly.

" This ar dumplings. My wife love them. Take it, You have it " I said. The minute I said. She looked at me.

Her eyes are moist. Her eyes widen.

" Thank... You sir " She said and took it. She quickly walked out of the room.

A tear rolled in my eyes.

She really looks exactly like Avery.

....

The night I came to resturant.

Why I want to see her again ?

I ordered food and waiting for her. My eyes rolled around. I didn't seen her anywhere.

I waited for past 3 hours. I helplessly walked towards washroom.

The minute I got out. Suddenly I heard a small whispers from girls washroom.

Is it good to peep in girls washroom. What if someone wants help ?

I walked inside. There I seen her.

Avery.... I mean Lisa.

She is having pain. She is on ground holding stomach tightly. My eyes widen in shock. I ran to her.

" Are you okay ? " I asked in worried tone. She just screaming in pain. I quickly lifted her in my arms. The walked out.

" Lisa " Suddenly I seen a same girl who gave me the address walked to me in worried.

" Inform her husband " I said quickly and started to walk. She walked behind me.

" Husband ? " She said.

" Yes.... What's his name ? Yes, John " I said quickly. She looked at me confusingly.

" GO !!! " I yelled. She nodded. I quickly walked out of the hotel. While my Assistant started the car. I placed her on back seat. I got inside. I placed her on my lap.

She is sweating and yelling badly in pain.

" GO FAST !!! " I yelled at John. He raised the engine.

She is holding tightly her belly. She closed her eyes tightly in pain.

" You are going to be ok " I said wiping her sweat. She hold my shirt tightly and buried her face on my stomach. She started to yell.

What I have to do ?

Suddenly I seen blood all over her thighs. My eyes widen in shock.

She is bleeding.

What do I do ?

" Jackson, How much time to reach the hospital ? " I asked quickly.

" Sir, It's traffic. It's take 30 minutes " He said.

30 minutes ?

My god !!! She will bleed to death.

First aid. I quickly pulled my phone and Googled it.

" Leads miscarriage"

My eyes widen in shock.

No, I lost my loved ones. I can do something to help a women in pregnancy.

" Jackson Close all the windows with shades. Even back of you " I said. He quickly done what I said.

The car is huge. I communicate with front seated with a small window. I told Jackson to close it. I don't want anyone to see.

" Ave.... Lisa " I called her. I took her face from my stomach.

" Open your eyes " I said. She is just yelling in pain. I seen the blood is all over the seat.

She is bleeding more. I quickly pulled out some tissues and my cotton clothes which are spare in my car. I quickly placed it under her.

Don't be ashamed Mike. She is pregnant lady.

" AH.... " I heard her large scream.

" Lisa, Hold my hand tightly " I said and took her hand she pressed my hand so tightly.

Why her touch make me familiar ?

Leave all this I have to save her and baby.

I placed my hand slowly on her bump.

What first aid should I give her ?

I quickly googled it. After I read.

" Lisa, Open your eyes. Look at me " I said. She didn't and yelling in pain.

A tear rolled in my eyes seeing her pain.

Why I am crying ?

" Lisa " I called. She didn't listen to me. Suddenly my phone buzzed.

Where did I put my phone ?

" Sir, Your phone is here " I heard jackson voice.

" Who is it ? " I asked looking at her and wiping her tears.

" Sir, It's little master Ron " He said.

I will call later.

Suddenly I seen Lisa opened her eyes and looked at me.

" Listen to me. Breath in. Breath out " I said quickly. She looked at me in tears.

" It... Pains " She said to me in tears.

I hold her hand tightly.

" Just do has I do ok ? " I said and showed her how to breath in and out. She tried and done what I said.

She relaxed a bit. I hold her belly.

The Google says the baby should be moving. But I can't sense anything.

Suddenly I heard her phone ringing. It says John. I quickly picked up.

" Lisa " He said on phone.

" I am taking her to xxxx hospital. Please come fast. Your wife is having severe pain " I said.

" Mike actually..... " Before he speak.

" When is her due date ? " I want to know to do some first aid.

" Due date ? She is 5 months pregnant " He said in worried tone.

She still have time then why she is bleeding and having this much pain.

" Mike it's... " He is about to say.

" I will talk to you later " I hung up the call.

Mike ? He knows my name.

He should've seen me on TV.

" AH... " She yelled. I looked down. The clothes got filled with more blood. Suddenly I seen she closed her eyes and felt unconscious.

" LISA !!!! " I yelled tapping her cheeks.

" Sir, we are here " Jackson said. He quickly opened the door. I covered her bottom with my jacket and lifted her and ran into the hospital.

" She is bleeding " Doctor said shockingly.

" Is it serious ? " I asked quickly.

" She will be miscarried " Doctor said. I eyes widen in shock. A tear dropped down my cheek and they quickly took her into Operation room.

That's the end of the chapter. Please do like, share and comment.

Guys please comment me. Don't be a silent readers.

Leave your comments I want to know how you guys feel about my book.

Hide

Mike point of view

I am chopping apples.

" Ah... " I heard a whisper. I quickly looked at her. She slowly woke up. I quickly walked to her.

" Are you okay ? " I asked and sat on bed.

" Baby " She said and quickly looked at her stomach.

Doctor said they struggled so hard to save the baby and her.

She placed hand on her stomach. She relaxed and closed her eyes.

" Eat apple " I said and took the plate and took the piece and placed it in front of her mouth. She looked at me confused.

" Where is my husband ? " She asked.

" John said to take care of you " I said. She looked at me in confused. She angrily threw the apple piece on ground.

" Who are you to take care of me ? I want to see my husband. Call him " She said angrily.

" First eat. I am going to make a call " I said. She looked at me angrily.

" Look, I resemble your wife. It doesn't mean that you can have feelings for me. I am married, this child is john's. My husband " She said angrily.

" I never said I have feelings for you. I never that the baby in your womb is mine. Why are you explaining to me ? " I asked.

That's all her face turned into shock.

" I.... Want to meet john " She said and about to get up.

" STOP ACTING AVERY !!! " I yelled angrily. She stopped and looked at me shockingly.

Few hours back.

I am standing in front of operation room.

God, Please don't let anything happen to them.

I don't know even she is not Avery. I just want them to be safe.

" Mike " Suddenly I heard a voice. As I turned around I seen John.

" She... Will be fine. " I am trying to comfort him. He walked to me.

" How is she ? " He asked.

" Doctor didn't came out " I said. John placed his hand on my shoulder.

" I... Am sorry Mike " John said sadly.

Why he is apologizing to me ?

I looked at him in confused.

" The.... Girl inside is your wife, Avery. She is carrying your baby " He said. My eyes widen in shock. A tear rolled in my eyes.

She is Avery. Then.... Lisa. They wedding photos.

" W_hat did you say ? " I confirmed.

" I just acted has Avery told me. I am sorry man " He said sadly.

" The photos of your wedding " I asked shockingly.

" It all set up " He said. My anger went out of extent. I pulled his collar angrily.

" You kidnapped Avery and you guys changed your names and now you are showing sympathy here. I know you black mailed Avery. " I said angrily. He looked at me shockingly.

" What are you saying ? " He asked in fear. I pulled his collar more tightly.

" DAMON !!! " I yelled angrily.

" W_ho..... is Damon ? " He asked. He can't able to breath.

He is still acting in front of me. I will kill you Damon.

I quickly punched on his face.

" MIKE, CALM DOWN " John yelled. Suddenly a nurse ran to us.

" Sir, it's hospital " She warned. I released his collar and hold my fist tightly in anger. She walked off. There I seen him on ground breathing heavily.

" Mike.... You misunderstood. I met Avery one month back. I am not Damon who you are taking about " He explained. I can't able to control my anger.

He is trying to safe himself.

I pulled his collar.

" I FOUND HER IN STREETS " He yelled sadly.

Streets ?

I loosen his collar.

" If you don't believe. I can prove you that I am not Damon who you are thinking. " He said and quickly pulled out the id cards and his proofs to me.

He looks decent guy. If he is not Damon. Where is that bastard ? What he done to Avery ?

" What happened ? " I asked.

" Can we sit and talk ? " He asked. I nodded we got seated.

" Yes, She told me to change her name. But... I am John. I am really John. I am not Dam....what's his name ? " He asked.

" Damon " i corrected.

" Ya!! Whatever he is. I am not him. " He explained.

" Main point " I asked seriously. He sighed.

" I met Avery on street. She is begging on roads in pregnant with her huge bump " He said.

My eyes widen in shock. My eyes filled with tears. Avery begged on roads.

" why...... She is begging on roads ? " I asked controlling my anger.

" Can you please let me complete ? " He said. I nodded.

" When I met her. I found her in a horrible state. She didn't eat for many days. I took her to my home and gave her food. We became friends. I asked her many times about her being like this. About her baby, About her husband. But.... She never told me. I told her to just rest. But... She didn't listened to me and found a job and started to work and leave in that stupid old building " John sighed.

My eyes widen shock and tears rolled down my cheek.

" One day, I found your wedding photo on her suitcase. That's why I know you. When I asked she accepted your relationship " John continued.

Past.

" Is your husband cheated you ? " I asked shockingly.

" No, He is good guy. He is the best husband I got in my life. " Avery said.

" Then... Why are you like this ? " I asked. She placed her head down. A tear rolled down her cheek.

" You are not going to say again " I said.

....

" She didn't explained me. Why she is in that state ? On that day. She suddenly called me quickly and told me to arrange all that. I got shocked to see you there. I want to say the truth but.... Avery stopped me. " John continued.

I placed my hand on head.

I shouldn't have stopped searching you. It's my fault.

" Did something happened between you Mike ? Who is this Damon ? " John asked.

I told him the entire story of Damon and Avery. John got shocked.

" Really ? Then is he alive right now ? Will he come back again to chase Avery ? " John started to throw questions.

" The only one who can answer this questions. Is Avery " I said. John nodded.

" Take care of her man. She lived a horrible 1 month. I don't know about 4 months. She always cried and thought of you. Cherish her " John said. I nodded.

" When you guys leave switzerland. Tell me, let's have dinner " John smiled. I nodded. He got up. We seen doctor came out. I quickly got up.

" How is my wife and baby ? " I asked wiping my tears.

" How can you let your wife work like that in pregnancy ? You almost lost your baby. We hardly tried and saved them. She is weak. Don't let her work. If this repeats. She will lead to miss carriage " Doctor said angrily. I nodded.

" Make her rest. She is just 5 months pregnant " Doctor said. We nodded. After doctor left.

" I told her to not work. I even gave her manger job in my hotel. She chooses cleaner. Stubborn women " John burst out angrily. I gave him a look.

" Sorry man " John said.

" You own the hotel I live right now " I asked. He nodded with a smile on his face.

He is rich too.

....

Tears started to flow down my cheek. I seen Avery shocked.

I walked to bed and sat beside her. I am about to take her hand she refused.

" Why are you doing this ? " I asked sadly. She didn't seen look at me once.

" I... Want to go " She is about to get up. I hold her hand.

" Where are you going ? Doctor told you to rest " I said.

" I.... Want divorce from you "

My eyes widen in shock. I controlled my tears.

" Give me a reason " I asked in tears.

" I.... I.... " She is trying to tell.

" Now, Don't tell me that you don't love me. I don't believe it. I have the letter you wrote. Don't even give me the reason of that bastard Damon. Don't even give me a simple excuses. Apart from all this say one reason " I said little angrily.

" Why don't you leave me ? " She said looking at me. There I seen her pale face and teary eyes. I am about to touch her face. She moved back. I controlled my tears.

" Why should I leave you ? " I asked in tears. She remained silent.

" What's making you leave me ? Is it because of that Damon ? What happened those 4 months ? " I asked angrily. She got up slowly. She is about to slip I hold her hand. She shook my hand.

" Why aren't you answering ? If it is him I am going to search him and kill him. " I said angrily and about to leave.

" HE IS DEAD " Avery yelled. I got shocked and turned to her.

" How ? " I asked. Again no answer.

Fine. Don't answer.

" If he is dead then what's the problem ? Why are you asking divorce ? " I said sadly. She didn't turned to me nor answering me.

" What are you hiding Avery ? " I said and walked and stood in front of her. She has tears in her eyes. Her eyes turned red.

I slowly took her face in my hands.

" He is dead. You suffered. I Suffered. Let's leave all this. Let's go to our home " I said in tears. She started to cry. She is crying so badly. I pulled her into a tight hug.

Seeing her crying looks like she was frozen all this month's and trying to melt all her tears.

....

" John brought your luggage. We are leaving tomorrow morning to america. Now, Let's go to hotel and rest " I said packing her stuff. She just sat on bed not responding anything.

I zipped up. I walked to her and about to help her to get up. Avery pushed me.

Fine. Be stubborn. I was once PYSCO too.

" Get up slowly " I said. She turned her head. I quickly lifted her in my arms.

" Put me down " She yelled angrily and trying to get down.

" DONT MOVE " I screamed angrily. She got scared and remained silent.

" It pains again. Don't move " I warned again. I walked out.

There I seen jackson stood.

" Bring the luggage " I said. He nodded.

....

The minute we reached my room. I hold her hand and made her sit on bed slowly.

The whole travel she didn't spoke to me nor looked at me.

Why aren't you saying what happened on those 4 months ?

Suddenly my phone buzzed. It's Ron. I looked at Avery and picked up the call.

" Pumpkin " I said.

Avery point of view

I won't let him know about the truth. I don't deserve them.

I got seated in bed. Suddenly Mike phone buzzed it's Ron. My eyes widen.

Ron, It's been a months since I spoke to him.

I missed him.

" I will be back tomorrow. I have a surprise for you " Mike said looking at me.

What he said all this days to ron ? How he convinced Ron ?

" Bye " He hung up the call.

I am hungry again. I just had breakfast.

I placed my hand on my belly.

" Are you hungry ? " Suddenly i heard Mike voice. I didn't respond to him.

From what I did those 4 months. I won't deserve to be with this people.

" Dumplings, Fish curry, Rice,..... " Mike kept on saying the dishes.

Is it for me or for whole floor people.

" Yes " He hung up the call. Suddenly I seen Mike started to walk towards me and sat on bed. I moved aside.

He just started to stare at me for past ten minutes. I just playing with my fingers.

" Why.... Are you wearing the torn dress ? " Mike asked looking at my hand which is torn. I quickly covered it with my hand. Mike got up. He pulled out a night Clothes.

" Change into this " He said. A tear rolled in my eyes.

How i spent those 4 months with ripped clothes on roads.

" Avery " Mike called. I took the dress. I moved slowly.

Ah... It pains.

" Don't get up. Let me help you " Mike said and about to hold me. I moved back.

" I.... Can change myself " I said a little angrily and about to get down. Mike hold my hand.

" Doctor told not to let you out of bed. You can have pain again. You can't stand, You bleeded badly " Mike said calmly.

" I can.... " Before I continue. Mike pulled the clothes. He slowly started to remove my buttons. My eyes widen in shock.

What he is doing ?

" Leave " I said and about to move.

" DON'T LET ME GET INTO A MONSTER AGAIN " Mike yelled angrily. I got scared. I seen his eyes are in pain, Guilt, Sorrow.

I can't able to see him like this. A tear rolled in my eyes.

He started to remove my shirt. I just sat there without saying a word.

I missed his touch, I missed when I use to be in his arms.

The minute he remove my clothes. His eyes landed on my bump. He stared I seen small tears are in his eyes.

His hands are shaking while he slowly touched my belly.

A tear dropped down his cheek.

" As promised..... You raised our baby " Mike said in tears. I can't able to control my tears and turned my head. Suddenly I felt his lips on my bump.

" I thought.... I lost you both " Mike said staring at my bump. He rested his head on my bump for a few minutes I didn't pushed him.

I just want to place my hand on his head and say " I love you " But.... I can't.

He got up and I quickly wiped my tears. Mike slowly wiped his tears and helped me get dressed. Before he get down from bed. He placed a small kiss on my forehead.

" I love you " He said looking into my eyes. I turned my head. He got up.

" Take rest " Mike said. I can see he don't want to cry in front of me. I walked to balcony.

There I seen him from reflection of mirror that he is crying badly.

I started to cry too.

I... Am sorry Mike. I have to hide this. I have to hide those 4 months. I feel ashamed for what I did.

....

I started to work. While I seen Avery beside me sleeping soundly.

She must be tired.

I smiled. I placed my one hand on her head and started to tap her with another hand I started to type.

I can't sleep. I... Am scared Avery will escape from me again. I won't let it happen.

" Ah... " Suddenly I heard a whisper. I looked at avery. She furrow her eyebrows.

Is she having night mare ?

" Avery ? " I called and hold her hand. I seen a pain in her face.

I have to submit this work tonight. I can't see Avery like this.

" I am here " I said pulled her closer with one hand.

" STOP !!! " Suddenly Avery screamed. I got shocked. I quickly placed the tab aside. I pulled her into my arms.

" It's mike..... Calm down " I said Rubbing her back with my hands. After a few minutes. She drift off to sleep. I pulled pillow and slowly made her lie on bed.

She is sweating. What she is dreaming ?

I wiped her sweat and gave a small kiss on her temple.

I smiled and pulled my tab again I started working again.

After a few hours. My back aches. I lie on bed and rolled to back and started to work.

" HELP ME !!! " Suddenly I heard Avery yelled again. I pulled her to me closely.

" It's fine. It's fine " I said and placed my arm on her and started to work.

Hey guys, I hope you like this chapter. Please do like, share and comment.

Let's wait how this couple going to have a end.

Back to home

A very point of view

I woke up. I didn't seen Mike beside me.

Where did he go ?

I got up slowly. I walked to living room there I seen him on sofa sleeping. There is files, papers, laptop spread all over the table.

He worked Last night. I didn't seen him working like this.

Without disturbing him. I slowly started to clean the table.

" What are you doing ? " Suddenly I heard this voice. He woke up. I quickly threw the papers on table.

" Don't work " Mike said while yawning and got up.

" I.... Am not helping you. I am searching my phone " I lied. Mike got up. He walked to the table beside bed and pulled my phone.

" Here " He gave me. I pulled the phone from him angrily. I walked to bed.

Is it fine to go to america with him. I decided to not look for him past few months.

But... Even if i refuse he will do what he has to do.

I seen Mike leaned on wall placed his hands in his pockets and started to stare at me.

I ignored him.I tried to lift my luggage.

It's heavy. I stopped. I placed my hand on stomach.

I started to breath heavily.

" Why did you stop ? Lift it " Mike said walking towards me. I looked at him angrily.

" Lift it , I want to see " He said angrily and fold his arms and stood in front of me.

You think I won't. I lifted more heavy weights past few months for my food.

But..... Right now I am weak. I can't able to stand . My legs are shaking.

I used my strength to lift. Suddenly I got out of balance and about to fall. A pair of arms wrapped around my waist.

" BE STUBBORN " Mike yelled. I am about to get out of his arms.

" Ah... My back " I whispered in pain holding my back.

" Sit here " Mike said making me sit on bed.

It pains badly.

Mike ran towards his luggage and pulled out a spray.

He carry pain killer spray.

He quickly sat beside me.

" Turn around " Mike said a little angrily.

" I... Can " I said in pain. He gave me a angry look. I silently turned around.

He slowly lifted my shirt a bit.

" Is it paining here ? " Mike asked pressing a little. I nodded as no.

" Here "

" A little left " I said in pain. He pressed.

" AH.... slowly " I got irritated in pain. He started to spray.

" Do you think you are Spider man ? Like You can lift anything " Mike said angrily.

I am having pain. He is scolding me.

" So, What if i am ? " I said irritatly.

" You are carrying a baby. Not a rice bag in your stomach " He yelled.

" I carried this rice bag and lifted more than this In past 3 months. It's just I am little weak right now " I said in irritated. Suddenly his hands got off me.

Why did I say to him ?

Mike turned me to him.

" You carried heavy bags in pregnancy. What exactly happened those months ? " Mike asked angrily and pulled my shoulders.

Yes..... I can't say it.

I placed my head down.

" No answer " Mike said sadly. He nodded.

" Fine. Fine. I will wait for the day to tell me. But.... Do whatever to escape, I will take you to our home. Get it ? " He warned. I just placed my head down.

" John invited to breakfast. Let's eat, we have flight at 12:00pm " Mike said.

....

" Lisa " Rose Ran to me and hugged me tightly.

We came to resturant.

I smiled.

Rose looked at Mike beside me.

" Hey, He is the man who asked your address. He looks scary " Rose whispered to me. I didn't answered her.

She loves John. They relationship is little complicated.

" Hey buddy, Thanks for coming " John said and there shake the hands.

We all got seated. While Mike sat me sit slowly on chair.

" Lisa, Who is he ? " There goes rose again. I looked at Mike.

" Her husband " Mike said.

She is going to kill you now.

" Bastard, you left her when she is pregnant. Do you know how she worked here ? You came to be with her again. I won't let it happen " Rose said angrily.

" Babe, Calm down. You don't know the entire truth " John got embrassed and pulling her hand to calm down.

" Calm down. He made Lisa life a hell " Rose said angrily. While Mike looked at me in confused.

" Sorry Mike. She don't know the truth " John apologized.

" Rose, First sit " I said angrily. She calm down and got seated.

" She is Avery " John said.

Rose eyes widen in shock.

" Avery ? Isn't it Lisa ? " Rose said shockingly.

It's embrassing. I don't know how Mike gone take all this.

" I.. will explain all when we get to home. Let's have breakfast" John made her calm. Suddenly a waiter came.

" Rose, Didn't I told you to wash dishes ? You are... " Before stopped seeing John.

" Master " She got scared and quickly bowed to him.

" She is my fiance. Not a worker, Go back to work " John said angrily. She nodded and ran from there.

" I told you to not work here has waiter. Look they think you are worker " John said little angrily.

" I want to convince your parents they are little mad at me " Rose said. John got frustrated.

" We are engaged. They... " Before he complete.

" Can we please eat ? " I interrupted.

" Yes, yes, let's eat " Rose quickly started to eat. I smiled.

" I... Will tell you when we get home " John said and started to eat.

We started to talk while I seen Mike just sat eating the food. It's looks like he doesn't exist here.

Ofcourse he is introvert.

I want to use washroom. I am about to get up.

" Where are you going ? " A quick question raised from Mike.

I won't escape don't worry. You won't let me. I can't ran too. It's better to be silent than running.

He hold my hand.

" I want to use washroom " I said. He quickly got up.

" I will come too " He said.

Excuse me. We have others too here.

Rose and John stared at us.

" I can go " I said a little angrily faking a smile.

" It's fine. Let me help you. Doctor told to not let you walk " Mike said.

He is making a crazy right now.

" I... " Before I argue further.

" Lisa... I mean Avery. Let me help you. Let's go " Rose said and stood up.

" NO !!! " Mike warned looking at her scarily. Rose zipped her mouth and quickly got seated and hide her face behind John.

" Babe, You don't know the situation. Let them handle " John said holding her hand.

" Fine " I said irritatedly. I am about to walk Mike placed his hand in my waist and hold my hand. I gave him a angry look.

We stood in front of washroom.

" Did you see rose got scared ? Why are you scaring people ? You were not this " I said angrily. Mike looked at me.

" Really ? Tell me the reason behind your divorce and those 4 months I will be back to be your old Mike " Mike said.

" You... " I raised my hand.

" Come on !!! Slap me. I am waiting. You give me my old Avery. I will give you old Mike Wilson " Mike said angrily.

He is making me angry. It's hard to win. Do whatever you want.

I am about to go inside Mike hold my hand tightly.

" Want to cheer me inside " I said. He quickly released my hand. Before I get inside. Suddenly Mike hold my hand.

" WHAT ? " I yelled angrily.

I am in hurry. I want to use the damn washroom. He is having fight with me here.

Looks like I started it. Stupid Avery.

" Please, Don't escape " Mike said sadly. I seen small tears in his eyes. I calmed down.

" I won't " I said. He released my hand. I walked inside.

....

" It's good to meet you Mike " John said shaking hand with mike.

" What's good ? He is scary " Rose whispered slowly and Mike heard it and rose quickly hide beside John. I smiled.

He looks scary. But... He is not.

" Rose, Shh...... " John made a smile to us.

" Thank you John " I said looking at John.

" Thank you ? Why I feel strange here ? " Rose asked sadly.

" Avery is leaving to America " John said. Rose shocked. She quickly ran to me and hugged me tightly.

" You are leaving " she cried. A tear rolled in my eyes.

They been my family this past one month. They treated me just like a family.

" Look after her. She Suffered a lot " John said sadly to Mike. Mike nodded and looked at me. We broke the hug.

" You have to attend our wedding. I will send you the invitation " John said. I nodded. I gave him a hug.

" Thank you " I whispered him and a tear dropped down my cheek.

If he didn't took me. I would've been in roads right now.

" He loves you. Tell him the truth. He will accept you. I want you to tell him the entire truth. He is really a nice guy. " John whispered to me slowly. A tear rolled in my eyes. We broke the hug while John smiled. I seen a small tears in his eyes.

" If you want any help we will always be there for you " Mike said. John nodded.

" When you visit switzerland. My hotel will always welcomes you " John said. We smiled.

Finally we said our goodbyes.

....

I stood in front of our home.

I never thought I would end up here again. It's looks like I came out of dead.

" Let's go inside " Mike said and took my hand. A tear rolled in my eyes. We walked inside.

We reached our floor. Mike opened the main door.

Every single thing is as it is. Our kitchen where we kissed. Living room where Ron and we use to have fun. Balcony where we had ice cream and a best night ever.

I started to explore the whole house. I am about to get upstairs.

" Wait !! " Mike stopped me and pulled my hand. I looked at him in confused.

" Don't take stairs. Come here " Mike took me to elevator. He pressed the button. We got inside.

" Till you deliver don't take stairs. Use elevator " Mike said.

He still loves me. I don't deserve him for what I did.

We came out of the elevator. We got inside our bedroom.

My eyes widen seeing the room. It is dark the curtains are closed. The minute Mike switched on the lights.

My eyes widen in shock. The room looks terrible. There is files, papers, laptop, election wires, gum, pins, pencils, pens......

Is it bedroom or a working place.

Every single thing used for working the business is in this room.

" I will call servant " Mike about to go.

" No, Let me clean " I said.

" Carrying that huge bump, are you going to clean ? " Mike said a little angrily.

I ignored him and about to take a step. Suddenly I kicked a bottle. I gave a look at Mike.

He is drinking.

" You get seated. I will clean " Mike said and took me and made a place on bed and made me sit.

He is about to go.

" When did you start drinking ? " I asked sadly placing my head down.

I feel guilty, because of me he became like this.

He didn't answered and walked off. A tear rolled in my eyes.

After a few minutes Mike came out wearing a normal night pants with a broom in his hand.

He looks cute with a broom in his hand.

He started to clean. While I slowly started to clean the bed.

" I told not to... " Before he complete.

" If you clean this huge room. I assure that I can't sleep tonight. I am just cleaning a small things. I want to take rest " I said angrily looking at him.

" Mean while sleep in Ron's room " Mike said in his angry tone.

Yes, where is Ron ? I forgot about him.

I didn't asked Mike about Ron. How can I ask him ? When I did such a terrible thing and got out of there life's.

I placed my head down and try to act like cleaning.

" Don't you want to ask about ron ? " Mike asked. A tear rolled in my eyes.

I want to know.

" You are angry with me not with Ron. Don't act like hating us. I know your feelings. " Mike said. I ignored him.

" He is in Ana's home. They will be here tomorrow morning. I didn't informed them that you are here. " Mike explained.

I want to see him badly. I want to hug him which I can't do. I want to meet Ana and stefen. I want to see there baby.

I missed so much.

" Whatever " I said and started to clean. I seen Mike controlled his anger and he too started to clean.

While I am cleaning Suddenly I found a book on a table.

My eyes widen seeing the book.

The title contains " MY LOVE "

The book has all my pictures in them. I looked at Mike who is busy in cleaning.

I placed it on table without asking him a question. I wiped my small tears.

After struggling for a hour. Finally we completed cleaning the room.

Mostly Mike cleaned it.

I seen the curtains.

He got addicted to dark again.

I pressed the button the curtains got opened. The room is filled with light.

I am about to get into the washroom.

" NO !!! " Mike yelled. My heart skipped a second. He blocked my way and stood in front of the door placing hands on both sides.

" I want to use washroom. I make sure I won't slip. We have dryer in bathroom one button the room gets dry " I said and about to take step.

" Use Ron's washroom " Mike said.

What he want ? Why we always stop me when I want to use washroom ?

" It takes time to go to his room. Get out of way " I said angrily. He still stood and made a smile.

I looked at him angrily.

" I want to use washroom badly " I said.

He is being stupid. He won't listen. I acted like I am having pain in my stomach.

" Avery " Mike quickly kneeled down. I got a chance and got inside quickly.

My eyes widen in shock seeing the bath room.

God !!!

Same files, papers , documents, books,pens.

Are you serious ? Is this a prank ?

Who uses all this in bathroom ?

" MIKE !!! " I yelled angrily. He came inside and gave a smile.

" I... Told you to not get inside "

I looked at him angrily.

" CLEAN " I yelled. He quickly started to clean.

Hey guys !!!

That's the end of the chapter. What do you think about this chapter ? Do you want them to be like before ? Or Do you love they fighting ?

Stay tuned for next chapter.

Please do like, share and comment.

Reunion

A very point of view

I felt someone licking my face. I woke up.

Sunny....

A smile appeared on my face. He grown up. He turned around waving his tail. I hugged him.

" I missed you " I said and placed kiss all over his face. He started to jump of me.

He looks happy to see me.

" Sunny , Get down " Suddenly I heard a voice. There Mike stood holding Ron in his hands.

" SIS !!! " Ron yelled loudly. Mike placed Ron on ground. He ran to me and quickly get on me and hugged me tightly.

" I missed you " A tear rolled in my eyes seeing him. I hugged him tightly. I can't refuse him. Ron broke the hug.

" Uncle told me he will bring you. Look he did it " Ron said smiling at me. I looked at Mike who stood there looking at us. Suddenly ron looked at my bump.

" Sis, You're fat " Ron said sadly. I chuckled.

" Sis is not fat. We are going to have a new family member soon " Mike said walking towards us. He got seated on bed.

" Really ? " Ron got excited. Mike nodded. Ron hugged me again.

Mike handled Ron every well.

I didn't spoke to him. I didn't asked him how is he ? Is he studying ? Is he eating properly ?

I just sat there like Ron is a stranger.

" Sis, we are going to play again, The Bed time Stories, The pan cakes you make, Movie, all going to come back " Ron said while smiling.

I just nodded.

" I will sleep with you tonight " Ron said.

" Hmm " I responded.

" Pumpkin, Sis has to take medicines. Go play with sunny downstairs " Mike said looking at me.

He is going to be angry with me.

The minute Ron walked out of the room. Mike slowly placed his hand on my face.

" Get fresh up. I prepared breakfast and.... " Before he continue. I removed his hand from my face. I am about to get down. Mike hold my hand.

" Let me help you " Mike said and about to place his hand on my waist.

" I CAN WALK " I yelled angrily. We started to stare.

" Avery... " Suddenly I heard a voice. As I turned to the direction. I seen Ana and stefen stood there.

They looked at my bump and got shocked. I placed my head down In embrassed.

How can I face them ?

Ana ran to me and hugged me tightly.

" Why did you ran away ? We searched you everywhere " Ana said in tears. A small tears appeared in my eyes.

" I... Am sorry " That's all come out of my mouth.

" Mike told us about that bastard Damon and all. Good he is dead " Stefen said.

" Mike told us you lived in Switzerland all this month's " Ana asked. I nodded in tears.

" You came back. Me missed you " Ana hugged me again.

" Where is my nephew ? I want to see him " I asked smiling at them.

" Just a minute. I will bring him right back " stefen said in excitement.

" Stefen, you guys go downstairs. We will be there. Let's have breakfast together " Mike said. They nodded.

" Baby has grown a lot " Ana said placing her hand on my bump.

I looked at Mike. Mike nodded and smiled.

he told them I am pregnant.

" Don't worry. We will tell you what to do in pregnancy. We are experienced " Stefen said. I nodded while smiling.

They went outside the room. Mike and I looked at each other. Suddenly I seen a small tears in his eyes.

" Let me help you " Mike said and hold my hand.

Why he is crying ?

He made me sit on a small table in bathroom.

" Here is soap, The towel, The shampoo, Hold this while showering. Don't step inside the bath tub. Its dangerous. I will bring your clothes " Mike started to explain. A tear rolled in my eyes. He is about to go. I hold his hand.

" Why are you crying ? " I asked sadly placing my head down. He quickly got kneeled in front of me. I looked at his red and teary eyes.

" You got happy when you met Pumpkin, Ana and stefen. You hugged them so warmly. Why are you not being with me just like old Avery ? Why are you being cold with me ? " Mike asked in tears.

I don't deserve you Mike.

I didn't answered him. Tears started to drop down my cheek.

" Whatever it is, I will accept. Just tell me. " Mike hold my hand in tears. I sat still not answering. Mike slowly placed his hand on my belly.

" Baby, Tell your mom to say the truth. Daddy loves mom. He can't see her like this " Mike said. I let out a cry.

I remembered the day when Mike said those similar words.

Baby, tell your mom to forgive me. Daddy loves mom. He can't leave without her

I started crying tears Started to flow down my cheek.

" I... Love your dad too " I said in tears. Mike looked at me shockingly and pulled me into a tight hug.

" I... Don't deserve you " I let out the pain. Mike broke the hug and wiped my tears.

" Why are you saying that ? " Mike asked.

I didn't answered him.

" I... Want to take shower " I said controlling my tears.

" I... Can't leave you like this while you are crying " Mike said in tears.

" Just go " I said and pushed him. Mike looked at me shockingly. He got up.

" I won't leave. I will stay here " Mike said. I just can't able to control my tears.

" Fine " I said angrily in tears. I started to remove my clothes. Mike turned his back quickly. I turned on the shower. I let out a cry.

" Please... Don't cry " Mike said. I just kept on crying placing my hand on my mouth. I just closed my eyes.

" Avery " Mike called. In a second I found him in my arms. We got wet in shower. Mike hugged my naked body tightly. He placed a kiss on my forehead. He hold my face in his hands.

" Don't cry. Doctor told you not to take stress " Mike said. I hugged him tightly.

Mike point of view

We all got seated for having breakfast.

Avery sat beside me.

" Let's cheers to avery's back " Ana said and raised her glass. We clicked the glass.

" Jack, Here aunty " Ana said holding jack in his arms. She came towards ana and gave him in her arms. I smiled looking at Avery.

" He grown up " Avery smiled placing her hands on his little face.

" How about we go on a trip for 2-3 days ? " Stefen asked.

" That sounds good " Ana Said and got seated. I looked at Avery.

I want to know is she want to go. I don't know what's happening to her. She not even speaking to be properly.

Why don't you say what happened those 4 months ?

" Mike ? " Stefen called. I came out of my thoughts.

" Yes "

" Let's go to coolest place. It will be awesome " Stefen said. I gave a look at Avery again. She just placed her head down.

" Sis, Select a place " Pumpkin said.

" Ron... It's... " Before ana speak.

" Come on Avery !!! We are back after a long time. Let's go on a trip. Do you know Mike use to be busy in work ever since you left him. He barley lives in this home. He always go to business trip. He became a..... " Before she go further.

" ANA !!! " Stefen Gritted his teeth and stopped her placing a hand on her palm.

Ana, Why are you saying all this ?

I placed my head down.

I don't want Avery to know all this.

" Ok, Let's go " Avery said. I got shocked and looked at her.

" Really ? " Ana said. Avery nodded.

" I... Want to use washroom " Avery said and Ana took jack in her arms. Avery got up slowly.

" Let me take you " I said. Avery didn't responded and started to walk slowly. I smiled at Ana and stefen.

" We will be back " I said.

" I am sorry Mike " Ana apologized.

" It's fine. She will be okay " I smiled. The minute I turned I didn't seen Avery. I quickly went to our bedroom. There I seen Avery stood in balcony. I slowly walked to her. I seen her wiping her tears.

" Don't take Ana's words. She just speaks randomly " I tried to make her calm.

" It's my fault. I pulled you out of the darkness and I dragged you into the darkness too " Avery said in tears. I quickly took her face in my hands.

" No... No, Now you are back. We are going to be a family again. Let's leave all the past and live happily forever " I said controlling my tears. She nodded as no.

" We can't go back to normal " Avery said and removed my hands from her. A pain hit in my heart.

" Why ? " I asked sadly. She didn't answered. I controlled my tears.

Avery point of view

Suddenly Mike hold his head tightly.

"AH .. " He yelled.

" Mike " I called and hold him.

" We... Love eachother. You can't leave me " Mike said suddenly I seen a vibration in his voice.

He looks different.

What happened ?

" Ok..... Ok.. " I made him calm.

" Who am I ? " Mike asked. My eyes widen in shock.

Suddenly I seen a vibration in his voice. In a second he ripped his shirt and started to see his tattoos.

" Mike... Mike... " I started to call him holding his hand. Suddenly Mike pushed me.

What's happening to you Mike ?

Tears started to roll down my cheek.

" My... Head is paining. What's happening to me ? " Mike said holding his head tightly.

" Mike, Look at me " I said holding his hand.

" What I did ? What's happening to me ? AH... " Mike yelled in pain. I hugged him tightly.

" Mike, Don't scare me " I said in tears. Mike broke the hug. He started to look at his tattoos.

" Avery.. left me. She left me " He started to speak to himself.

Panic started in me. My heart started to beat fastly.

" Mike, I am here " I hold his face. Mike looked into my eyes.

" No, You are not Avery " He pushed my hands. My eyes widen in shock.

" Mike, I am scared " I said in tears.

" My... Wife is pregnant " He said in vibration.

Mike turning into PYSCO. I can't let him be go into that again.

" Look. I am pregnant " I said showing him the bump in tears. He looked at bump in tears.

" My.... Baby. But... Avery left me. You are not Avery. She left me. She don't like me. She left with Damon " Mike said in tears and vibration.

What's happening Mike ?

I am scared. Don't do this.

" No, I am back. I killed him. I killed him. He won't come to us. I will be with you always " I said in tears and hugged him tightly.

" You... Killed Damon " Suddenly I heard Mike voice. I broke the hug.

" Yes... Yes.. I killed him. I won't leave you. Don't become the monster again. Please... Please... " I said in tears.

" This is the reason you are avoiding me " Suddenly Mike said. I furrowed my eyebrows. My eyes widen in shock.

He just turned into PYSCO right ?

" You... Just acted " I said angrily and moved back.

" You are avoiding me just for this " Mike asked sadly. I placed my head down. Mike came to me and pulled my shoulders.

" DON'T BE SILENT AVERY " Mike yelled angrily. My heart skipped a bit. Tears started to roll down my cheek.

" Avery, I am asking you " Mike yelled again. I just turned my head.

" Just this small reason and you are avoiding me and hiding from me from past 5 months " Mike asked sadly.

" It's Not a small reason. I killed a person " I said angrily in tears looking at him.

" He deserve it " Mike said. My eyes widen in shock.

" I am a murderer Mike. I been in jail for 2 months " I said in tears. Mike eyes widen in shock.

" Jail ? "

I can't able to take this I am about to go. Mike pulled my hand.

" Don't escape Avery. We are not done yet " Mike said angrily.

" We can't let our friends wait like that. Let's go " I diverted.

" Avery for God sake. Please tell me " Mike requested in worried. I am about to go again. Mike pulled my hand again.

" I won't let you go. Till you split out the truth " Mike said angrily.

" What do you want to know ? " I asked angrily.

" What. Happened. Those. 5. Months ? " Mike mentioned every word deeply in anger.

" Yes, I killed him. I am murderer. The cops arrested me. The case continued for 1 month and they released me. Got it. Fine " I said controlling my tears. Mike got shocked.

" Didn't you thought of me for a second ? I would've helped you. Why playing this hide and seek ? Why did you tortured yourself and baby so much that you end up in roads ? Did you even forget that you were a rich man's wife ? " Mike said angrily in tears.

" It's my life. It's my body. It's my baby " I said angrily. Mike released my hand.

" My baby ? " Mike nodded and moved back. A pain hit in my heart.

I.... Am sorry. I... Am sorry. I didn't told you the entire truth.

" I... Never thought you will say my baby " Mike said sadly in tears. I turned my head and pressed my mouth tightly to control my tears.

Without speaking any further Mike walked off without turning back.

I started to cry standing there. I placed my hand on my stomach.

I won't deserve him.

....

" Canada, It's fix " Ana yelled. We are seated on sofa discussing about trip. While Mike didn't even looked at me.

You should be happy that he is ignoring you then why are you waiting for this response ?

" Avery, what do you think ? " Suddenly I heard Avery voice.

" Whatever you decide " I said and smiled.

" Sis, ice cream " Suddenly Ron asked who sat on my lap.

" It's in fridge. Go get it " Mike ordered angrily. I looked at him. While ana and stefen got shocked for his behaviour. Ron got scared and hide his face in my chest.

" Mike, Why did you tell at Ron ? " Stefen asked in confuse. Mike didn't responded.

" Let me get you " Ana about to get up.

" I am thristy. I will have water anyway. I will get it " I said controlling my tears and placed Ron on floor and about to go. Ron clenched my dress. I turned around.

" I will come too " Ron said with little voice. A tear rolled in my eyes. I nodded while smiling and took his little hand and we walked towards the kitchen.

" Mike, Are you insane ? " I heard Ana started scolding Mike.

" He is really stupid " Stefen said angrily. The minute I got into kitchen. I opened the fridge. I let out a cry silently.

" Sis, Chocolate ice cream " Ron said pointing to the ice cream. I quickly wiped my tears. I took the ice Cream.

I took some ice cream in a cup and gave it to ron. He took it and Started to eat happily. I smiled looking at him.

It's been a long time since I spent time with him.

" Delicious ? " I asked tapping his head. He nodded and walked out of the kitchen.

Why I am disliking when Mike is being cold to him ?

It's the same thing I wanted from him.

Why i am having pain in my heart ?

" Avery " Suddenly I heard Ana voice. I quickly threw the spoon on ground and acted. I am about to bend.

Shut !!! I can't bend. I wiped my tears.

" Let me take it " Ana picked up the spoon. I smiled.

" Are you okay ? " Ana asked and hold my arms. I nodded quickly.

" Mike must be stressed from work. Don't take it to heart. He loves Ron. " Ana said sadly.

" I know " I smiled. Ana looked at me in my eyes.

" Is everything ok between you two ? " Ana asked.

" Yes, Everything is fine. He is just a little angry that I didn't take medicines. We are fine. Don't worry " I lied patting his palm. Ana exhaled.

" My god !!! I was worried. Me and stefen got panicked to see you too being awkward ever since we seen you " Ana said. I smiled.

" So, How about a shopping for a trip ? We are leaving day after tomorrow " Ana said in excitement.

Will it be awkward between us in trip ?

" Ok " I nodded.

....

It's mid night. Mike went to work and back. He is still working in bed room.

Ana said never since I left he got involved in work.

Should I make some coffee ?

I got up slowly walked to kitchen and prepared coffee.

I am about to leave. Suddenly my legs got numb.

Ah... Why legs got numb ?

I can't able to take step.

I hardly took small steps and reached elevator and got Inside.

I walked slowly into the bedroom holding cup of coffee.

I seen mike working seated on bed. I walked to him and placed the coffee on table. Mike didn't gave a look at it.

I walked to other side on bed and got seated. I closed my eyes in pain.

I bent down to touch my legs. I can't reach on my legs.

Mike point of view

" Uncle, Our plan worked " Pumpkin ran to me holding sunny in his hands. I smiled.

" Keep him down " I said. Ron placed sunny on floor and jumped into my arms.

" Is sister still angry with you ? " Pumpkin asked. I nodded sadly.

I planned that to be cold to avery. I am sure she will relieve her true self. I involved Ron so it will easier when she sees Ron unhappy.

When I be cold. I am sure she will be angry and comes to me.

" Let's continue the plan. Don't feel sad when I scold you ok ? " I said sadly to pumpkin.

" It's promise. It's plan uncle. We will bring sis back " Ron said smiling at me. I hugged him.

He is really grown up.

" It's late. Go to sleep " I said. Ron nodded and quickly walked out of the room.

I opened my laptop. I seen in camera that Avery is in downstairs making something in kitchen. I smiled

I got relieved. I started working.

After a few minutes. I seen Avery walked into the room holding a coffee in her hand. She placed it on table. I didn't gave a look at her.

I smiled inside. I slowly looked at Avery. Suddenly I seen she is trying to hold her legs. Because of her bump she can't able to bend.

Is she okay ?

" Ah... " Suddenly I heard a whisper. I turned my side to avery.

" What happened ? " I quickly asked her. She nodded as no in pain.

Stubborn girl.

I quickly got down the bed and ran to her and kneeled in front of her. I looked at her pale face. She closed her eyes in pain.

" Are you okay ? " I asked and placed my hand on her bump. She quickly nodded as no.

" Is it paining ? " I asked in worried.

" My.... Legs... I can't able to move " Avery said in pain.

Can't move ? What happened ?

I quickly ran to my mini fridge and pulled out the water and heated it.

Water got warmed. I placed it in front of her.

" Put your legs here " I said and hold her legs and placed it in tub.

" Is it okay ? " I asked. She nodded as yes. I started to press her legs slowly.

After a few minutes of pressing her legs. Suddenly I seen Avery drozed. I smiled. I removed her legs slowly.

I slowly sat beside her.

"Are you sleepy ? " I asked. She nodded and in a second she slept on my shoulder. I smiled. I slowly made her sleep on bed.

I got on other side of bed. I seen Avery sleeping soundly. I slowly removed her hair locks behind her ear.

I will bring you back Avery.

I slowly placed my hand on her stomach.

You grown a lot baby. When I seen you, you were not shown yet. Now see you look huge.

Don't hurt mom, Don't trouble mom, let her rest, ok ?

" Hmm " Avery suddenly turned to other side. Suddenly I seen her moving from one side to other.

Is she can't able to sleep ?

" What happened ? " I asked moving closer to her.

" I... Can't sleep properly " Avery said in her sleep. I looked at her bump.

Oh !!! She can't sleep properly because of bump.

I took her face and made her sleep on my shoulder and pulled her closer to my side.

It's been 5 months since I slept with you like this.

I slowly placed a pillow below her waist.

" Is it okay now ? " I asked. She nodded. I smiled.

Good night Avery.

Good night baby.

I placed my hand on her bump and closed my eyes.

Please do like, share, comment.

Trip

Mike point of view

" Yeh.... We are in canada " Pumpkin yelled loudly the minute we got out of the airport.

Avery sat beside me. She is sleeping on my shoulder.

She must be tired.

After a few minutes we reached our hotel.

Avery woke up. We got down and took out all the luggages.

" Let me fill the details " Stefen said and walked inside. I nodded and we got inside the hotel.

I looked at Avery. She not spoke a word on our travel.

We cleared out misunderstanding. Why are you behaving like this ? It's not your fault. He deserved it.

" Mike, Here is your room key " Stefen handed me the key.

We walked to our rooms.

" Uncle, I love this place " Pumpkin said in excitement holding the toy in his hand.

" Really ? " He nodded quickly. I turned to avery. She got seated on bed.

It doesn't look like a trip when she is being like this.

I signal to ron about our plan to start. He nodded while smiling.

Ron quickly walked to the luggage and started to pull out the clothes.

" PUMPKIN !!! " I yelled.

Here comes our acting skills.

Avery quickly gave attention to us.

" You are messing the room " I said angrily. Pumpkin placed his head down sadly.

Wow !!!! He should be actor.

" I.... Am hungry. I want to eat chocolates " Pumpkin said sadly.

" Didn't I told you to be disciplined "

I gave a look at Avery.

Why isn't she responding ?

" Go, Take bath " I said angrily. Ron sat there without moving a step.

Me and pumpkin are eagerly waiting for her response.

Don't be like this Avery. Be like a normal person. Talk to us, Fight with us, Scold us like you usually do.

" NO !!! I WILL EAT CHOCOLATE " Ron yelled loudly.

" You are raising your voice in front of your uncle " I yelled angrily and about to go to him.

" Ron, Come here " Avery said in low tone tapping on bed.

I smiled inside.

Ron walked to Avery and got seated beside her.

" Listen to uncle " Avery said looking at Ron.

What ? That's it.

Don't you scold me ?

Where is my old Avery ? You love Ron more than me. Why aren't you taking side of him ?

" I... Don't like uncle. He is scolding me always " Ron said sadly.

That's a good line. I should give him a award.

Avery looked at me.

" Just listen to uncle " Avery said a little angrily.

" NO !!! I HATE HIM " Ron yelled loudly. Suddenly Avery gave a slap on Ron's little cheek.

My eyes widen in shock. Ron started to cry.

I ran to Ron and quickly pulled him in my arms. I looked at Avery. She just turned her head.

What kind of stupid behaviour is this ?

She is really not my avery ?

What's your problem Avery ? We cleared everything.

You said my baby. Now, You slapped Ron.

Why you are making us hate you ?

" What is this behaviour ? Me and ron planned all this just to make you bring back. Why are you being this cruel ? " I asked angrily tapping Ron's back who is crying badly.

She didn't answered and walked out.

I sat on bed holding Ron. I looked at his teary eyes.

" Shh... Don't cry. I... Am sorry. I brought you in this mess " I said sadly wiping his tears.

" She... Is not my sis " Pumpkin said in sobs. I pulled him into a tight hug. A tear rolled in my eyes.

After struggling for a hour. I made him sleep. Suddenly I heard a sound from living room. I ran towards there only to see Avery got dressed up and about to going out.

I quickly pulled her hand.

" Where are you going ? " I asked angrily. She removed my hand.

" I want to take some fresh air " She said angrily looking at me.

" Do you know this place ? What if you get lost ? It's freezing outside. Don't be stubborn. Get inside " I said angrily. She about to open door. I stopped her.

" Ron is sleeping, Don't make me yell " I controlled my anger.

" He is your responsibility. You handle him " Avery said angrily. My eyes widen in shock. I can't able to control my anger.

" Come with me " I said angrily and pulled her wrist and took my jacket.

" Leave me " She said removing my grip. I gave her a angry look. Avery got scared. I opened the door and locked it.

Avery point of view

The pain I am going through you won't get it Mike.

I deserve you all. You may be taking it as easy but I killed a person and I... I...

" Today you have to answer all the questions " Mike dragged me outside of the hotel.

The cold breeze hit me. We got inside the car.

Soon we reached a place.

It's so cold here. I placed my hands into my pocket to keep myself warm.

I looked around, there is snow every where.

Mike dragged me into the snow.

" It's cold. Where are you taking me?"

I said angrily. He made me stand in snow.

" Come on !!! Take fresh air. I will be waiting " Mike roared angrily. I seen a anger and red eyes.

I hold my stomach. I can't able to stand in snow. I am freezing completely.

" Why are you punishing me ? " I asked angrily. Mike chuckled.

" Punishing ? You deserve for what you did to Ron few minutes back " He yelled angrily.

Yes, I deserve it.

" Why are you being like this ? I told you I don't mind killing that bastard. I don't mind you went to jail. You are not murderer. You don't need to walk far away from us " Mike said sadly.

I am about to go. Mike pulled my wrist.

" WE ARE NOT DONE " Mike yelled angrily pulling me closer to his chest.

" You have to answer today " Mike said on my lips.

We are freezing and the cold air is letting out of our mouths.

" I am freezing " I barley spoke. He hold me tightly.

" Answer " He said angrily looking into my eyes.

I can't able to stand. My legs got numb. My eyes are closing slowly. My lips got dry. My heart started to beat fastly.

" Please.... Let me go " I said in low tone.

" Answer "

Slowly my eyes started to close. Mike just looking at me. He is being stubborn just like me.

" You are carrying baby. Answer me quickly. You can't make it. You are about to get unconscious " Mike said holding me tightly.

Baby.... No... I can't let anything happen to our baby.

" What.... You.... Want to know ? " I said in low tone.

" You know what to answer. Don't make me repeat Avery " Mike said.

No.... I won't tell you. I feel disgusted.

" Mike.... Baby... Please " I begged small tears appeared in my eyes. I started to close my eyes slowly.

" 5 minutes left " Mike said looking into my eyes. I chuckled.

" Do you think by doing I will tell the truth ? Never " I smiled. Mike smiled.

" Do you think I care for baby ? We can have another. Right now I want most is truth. Even if you don't tell the truth the one who suffers is baby not you " Mike said angrily.

My eyes widen in shock.

No.... I lived all this days just for my baby. If the baby is harmed I can't live.

Mike does anything to make me spill the beans.

When he says he don't care about the baby. He actually does what he say.

He chooses me more than baby.

" 1 minute " Mike counted. My eyes started to close soon.

My body got cold. I completely now got collapsed on Mike. Mike hold me tightly.

" Remember if doctor tell me to choose one. I will choose you. Now it's your choice to save the baby or not " Mike whispered in my ear.

" 10 ..... 9 ..... 8.....7....6.. 5.... 4.... 3... 2..."

" I....was raped "

I got unconscious in his arms.

Mike point of view

My eyes widen in shock. In a second. I quickly lifted her in my arms. I ran towards the car.

" ON THE HEATER !!! " I yelled at driver. He quickly switched on. The car started to get heated up.

" PUT WINDOW SHADES.

GET OUT !!! " I yelled.

" Yes... Sir "

I walked out. I quickly removed my shirt. I started to remove Avery's clothes.

" Get up... Please " Tears rolled in my eyes.

We are completely naked. I pulled her into a tight hug. I started kiss her forehead, cheeks, Neck to make her warm. I pulled the seat back.

I made her lie on seat. I hugged her tightly and started to rub her.

The car got so heated that I started sweating.

Get up.... Please. This is the only way to make you tell the truth. I don't want to regret again for taking this step.

Please get up. I don't want you two to harm.

I am trying hard to make her warm.

" Avery... Get up " I said tapping her cheeks.

A tear dropped from my eyes.

" Look... It's mike " I seen her eyes closed.

I should've not done this.

In a second I gave a kiss on her lips. I started to kiss her. I looked at her. Avery started sweating.

It's working. I slowly kept on kissing her. I completely got wet in sweat.

" Hmm " Suddenly I seen Avery responded to my kiss. My eyes widen. I just got more passionately. Her hands got around my neck.

She is awake.

" Hmm.. " Avery tapped my back. She is struggling now to get out of my grip. I stopped kissing and looked at her.

" I... Can't breath " Avery said. She opened her eyes. I got relief. Tears rolled down my cheek. I pulled her into tight hug.

You are alive. I thought you won't wake up.

I quickly broke the hug and kissed her all over the face.

" Mike "

" Get up slowly " I made her get up. I quickly pulled her dress and helped her to get dressed.

I too got dressed up.

I pressed the buttons seats for set.

I quickly pulled out the hot soap from the box.

I prepared all this. I don't want Avery to get cold and I don't want my baby to harm.

" Quickly have this " I said making her eat. I started to wipe her sweat while feeding her.

" Mike " Before she speak.

" Shh.... For few minutes please don't speak " I requested. I knocked the window.

Driver got signal. He got inside and started the engine. I pulled Avery closer. I placed my hand on her forehead.

Thank god !!! She don't have fever.

" Mike " Avery tried to speak again.

"Please.... " I requested rubbing her hands.

After a few minutes. We got inside the hotel.

" Yes, Doctor is waiting " A man said. I nodded Avery is in my arms.

The minute we got inside the room. I quickly placed Avery on bed.

" Doctor, Check her " He started to check.

Please.... Tell me both are fine.

" She is fine " Doctor said.

" What about baby ? " I asked quickly.

" Baby is fine too. She just have a light fever. I will prescribe some medicines. Don't let her be in cold "

I Exhaled. I nodded.

I sent doctor outside.

Avery point of view

I seen Mike walked to me quickly. He sat beside me.

" Are you okay ? Is it paining ? " Mike asked in worried and placed his hand on my stomach. I just started to stare at him.

Why did you go this peak to spill my truth ?

Tears rolled in my eyes.

" Take rest " Mike said removing my hair locks.

Why don't he ask about what I told him ?

He covered me with blanket and about to go. I hold his hand. Mike turned to me.

" Sleep " He smiled and before I speak. He walked out.

Why isn't he asking anything ?

....

What's happening here ?

Don't he want to ask me anything ?

He done this far to spill the truth and he isn't asking me anything.

I got slowly. I walked towards the balcony there I seen him looking at the stars. I walked to him slowly.

" Mike " I called him. He quickly turned to me.

" I told you to rest " Mike said coming towards me and hold my hands.

" Mike... " Before I continue.

" Go back to bed " Mike took my hand and about to take me inside. I stopped him.

" We have to talk "

" You have a mild fever. Get inside " Mike said he about to take me inside. I stopped him.

" IT'S COLD HERE " Mike yelled angrily he quickly took me inside. He made me sit in bed.

" Lay down " I nodded as no in tears. I can see he is trying to control his anger.

" You want to know the truth, You got it. Why are you avoiding me ? Am I disgusting ? " I asked in tears. Mike eyes widen in anger.

" I am angry. I will speak to you when I cool down. Right now sleep " Mike said angrily looking at me. I got up.

" Are you angry because.... I was raped ? " I asked in tears.

" SHUT UP !!! " Suddenly I heard his scream. I moved back in fear. Mike turned his back in frustration.

" I......don't deserve you. I.......Was raped " I said in tears placing my head down.

" How can you decide that I don't deserve you ? Do I say to you when you are raped I don't want you ? " Mike bursted in anger. Tears started to flow down my cheek. I took his hands.

" It's... Not that. I... Am not pure. I... Am disgusting " I said in tears. Mike looked at me in tears.

" ENOUGH !!! " Mike yelled. I shivered.

" I don't want to hear that again " Mike said angrily pointing his finger to me.

" Do you know how I felt you are not speaking to me ? Do you know how I felt when you said it's your baby ? Do you think this thing makes difference in our relationship ? Do you think I won't accept you ? " Mike said sadly in tears. I quickly took his hands.

" I... Am sorry. I should've told you. I was scared. I thought I don't deserve you " I said in tears. In a second Mike pulled me into a tight hug.

" I... Am sorry that I didn't protect you " Mike said sadly. I hugged him tightly and started to cry.

" Don't be guilty. Don't be disgusted. You are always pure in my heart " Mike said. I pulled him more tightly.

" You must be scared right ? " Mike asked. I nodded in tears. Mike pulled me more closer.

After a while Mike broke the hug. He slowly wiped my tears. I seen his eyes are filled with tears too.

He just started to stare at me.

" I missed my avery " Mike said in tears.

I just kissed his lips slowly Mike responded.

We started to kiss. Mike pulled my waist. We started to kiss deeply like we are waiting for this.

Suddenly Mike lifted me and placed me on the piano. He stared at me.

" Which place do you want to visit in canada ? " Mike asked removing my hair locks behind my ear.

" Hmm " I started to think. Mike smiled.

" Uncle " Suddenly we heard pumpkin voice. We turned to him. There he stood wiping his eyes. Mike moved back a little.

How can I face him now. I slapped him.

I just placed my head down.

" Pumpkin " Mike walked to him and quickly lifted him in his arms.

I tried to get down. But... I can't able to get down.

Mike came to me. I can't able to meet my eyes with Ron.

" Pumpkin, Sis wants to say something to you " Mike said and raised his eyebrows to me.

" I don't want to talk with sis " Ron said and hugged Mike tightly without seeing me. A pain hit in my heart tears rolled in my eyes.

" Pumpkin, Look here " Mike made Ron to look at me. He didn't turned. Mike hold my hand.

A tear dropped down my cheek.

" Oh !!! Look sis is crying " Mike said. Ron quickly turned and looked at me.

" I... Am sorry Ron. I promise i won't hit you again " I said in tears. Ron jumped into my arms.

" Slowly " Mike smiled making sure I am fine. I nodded. He hugged me tightly. I smiled in tears.

" Who wants to eat ice cream ? " Mike asked.

" ME " Ron quickly raised his hand. We laughed. We had a group hug.